PRAISE FOR
COURTNEY ELIZABETH MAUK

The Special Power of Restoring Lost Things

"Can we ever let our children go? That's the question that Courtney Elizabeth Mauk asks in her riveting novel *The Special Power of Restoring Lost Things*. Heartbreaking in its close observation of how each person's grief is a world unto itself, Mauk's novel plunges us into loss but also reveals—in tense, evocative prose—the ways grief connects us through its filaments of need. We learn what it's like to miss something so intensely—through fragments of past conversations that mingle with the present and, in one exquisitely drawn scene, through the brushing of an absent daughter's hair—that we can almost cross that thin, forbidden membrane that separates the living and the dead."

—Scott Blackwood, author of *See How Small*

"*The Special Power of Restoring Lost Things* is a compelling portrait of a family caught in a terrible limbo. Mauk draws her characters with insight and sensitivity, weaving a suspenseful tale of a young woman's disappearance and the chaos and pain left in her wake. A chilling, beautiful novel."

—Cari Luna, author of *The Revolution of Every Day*

"A wise, moving, and suspenseful tale of a New York family struggling to cope in the aftermath of trauma, *The Special Power of Restoring Lost Things* reveals chilling complexities of maternal love and parental loss."

—Helen Klein Ross, author of *What Was Mine*

"*The Special Power of Restoring Lost Things* deftly examines the emotional and psychological repercussions for a family left behind by a disappeared daughter. Courtney Elizabeth Mauk paints a powerful portrait of grief, dread, distrust, and—ultimately—redemption as mother, father, and brother try to make sense of a bereft world."

—Miranda Beverly-Whittemore, author of *June* and *New York Times* bestseller *Bittersweet*

Orion's Daughters

"Mauk's follow-up to her debut . . . revolves around the enduring bond between two girls raised in a commune in Ohio . . . Mauk's second venture is a nuanced character study that draws the reader into its compelling, unique world."

—*Booklist*

"A spectacular evocation of isolation and idealism—and the danger of pursuing both with too much ardor. Courtney Elizabeth Mauk is an exquisite, sharp-eyed stylist and *Orion's Daughters* is a gorgeous meditation on the enduring power of friendship and what happens to a person when the ghosts of their childhood threaten to overwhelm them."

—Laura van den Berg, author of *The Isle of Youth* and *Find Me*

"It's clear to me that Courtney Elizabeth Mauk is going to be an important new voice of her generation."

—Dan Chaon, author of *Await Your Reply* and *Stay Awake*

Spark

"[Mauk] writes skillfully about the sibling bond between Andrea and Delphie, setting their new life in a layered New York landscape . . . Subway riders, trendy Brooklynites, urban children—all come to life with precision through the lens of Andrea's lonely eyes."

—Elizabeth Word Gutting, the *Washington Post*

"A riveting read that will keep the pages turning, highly recommended."

—*Midwest Book Review*

"In *Spark*, Courtney Elizabeth Mauk has somehow managed to write a book that's both chilling and heart-rending. It's a masterfully unnerving portrait of dissolution: of a family, of a life, of a mind. Her artfully distanced prose gets under your skin like little else. After you pick this book up, it won't put you down."

—Kelly Braffet, author of *Josie and Jack* and *Last Seen Leaving*

THE SPECIAL POWER OF RESTORING LOST THINGS

THE
SPECIAL
POWER
OF
RESTORING

A NOVEL

LOST
THINGS

COURTNEY ELIZABETH MAUK

Published by Little A, New York

www.apub.com

Amazon, the Amazon logo, and Little A are trademarks of Amazon.com, Inc., or its affiliates.

ISBN-13: 9781503937055 (hardcover)
ISBN-10: 1503937054 (hardcover)
ISBN-13: 9781503937062 (paperback)
ISBN-10: 1503937062 (paperback)

Cover design by Faceout Studio

Printed in the United States of America

*For the girls
and their families*

One

Carol pictured somewhere larger, louder, a place where getting lost would be a common mistake. Instead she finds a small, dark room outlined in red—a predictable color scheme, but she likes it, the sexy mood it creates. She can imagine her daughter leaning into the bar, the tiny red lights along the edge reflecting onto her pretty face, her slick lips, red too, pulling back as she smiles. Her strong teeth, aligned by eighth-grade braces, the clear kind, which she'd begged Carol to let her have. There would be an eager shine to Jennifer's eyes—all those expansive hours ahead, the promise of adventure. Why should she have thought that night would be any different?

It's a Thursday, but Carol still expected more of a crowd. She pulls at the skirt, which strikes her now as embarrassingly short. For over a month, she has been able to fit into Jennifer's clothes, yet every time the ease surprises her. The skirt she knew was a stretch the moment she put it on, although in the hallway mirror she was impressed by how good her legs looked. The blouse is white silk, a caress against the skin. She had to achieve a precarious balance: she wanted to get inside the club door, but she didn't want to be laughed back out.

Impulsively, she undoes the blouse's top two buttons. She's not sure how to do this anymore.

At the back she finds an area for dancing. In Jennifer's honor, Carol stands in the center of the empty floor and closes her eyes, lets her body sway to the music. She tries to move as Jennifer would: unself-consciously, with joy. Her muscles stiffen. When she looks up, the DJ is watching her. Despite the tight T-shirt and spiked hair, his lined face marks him as an imposter. Like the Rolling Stones, grandfathers cavorting onstage past their bedtime, an embarrassment. He should give it up before it's too late, hand over youth to those who deserve it.

She tugs at her skirt. What she's doing is different.

A year has passed. Time has never moved more slowly, yet the implausibility of a full year without Jennifer astounds her. Carol doesn't think she can live through another.

As she dances, she looks for her daughter. For that blond head, the shape of which she knows as well as her own. For those narrow shoulders that hike up when she laughs. For the profile that will take Carol's breath away: her heart, separated, beating here.

At the bar she orders a kamikaze, Jennifer's drink. The bartender is young and lovely, her skin pale, her head a cascade of dark curls. She wears a black tank top, the club's name, Inferno, emblazoned across her chest in silver sequins.

"Have you worked here long?" Carol asks, but the bartender is turning around, fiddling with the register screen.

The DJ switches songs—a high male voice swooping and falling through the beat like a trapped bird. On the bar, a votive candle casts odd shadows onto Carol's hands. She picks the candleholder up, twirls it around, pours a drop of wax onto her wrist. The sting is there and gone, leaving almost no trace of its memory. In Jennifer's apartment they found candles on top of the coffee table, the bookshelves, the windowsills, the back of the toilet, the wicks burned down low. Brightly colored candles with garish images of Jesus, the Virgin of Guadalupe, Saint Francis, and Saint Jude. Carol can't guess why they were there, for art or salvation. She has no idea what prayers might move her daughter's lips or where she could have learned them.

The bartender looks over her shoulder, scanning the bar for business.

"My daughter comes here," Carol says, raising her voice. "Jennifer. Her last name is Bauer."

The bartender blinks.

Carol puts her drink down with more force than she intended. She clenches her hand at the impact.

"Another?" the bartender asks.

Carol nods. She has come here for this purpose: to drink, to get drunk, to reclaim her beating heart.

Two

Fight your battles, Drew tells himself as his wife slips out of bed. *Let her go.*

For two hours, unable to fall asleep, he has been lying on his side, staring through the darkness at the closed blinds, going over tomorrow's agenda. He likes picturing each entry in his phone's calendar, a division of the day into orderly steps, one purpose, one accomplishment, after another. Usually, like counting sheep, the ritual slips him seamlessly under, but not tonight. Every time he tries, the hole in tomorrow's agenda remains, plunging him downward.

When Carol came to bed at eleven, he evened out his breath. She hovered over him before flopping down and pulling the sheet over her head. But as soon as he drifted toward the edge of sleep, one of her sighs, her twitches, brought him back. He could picture her eyes wide open, staring. An hour later, when the mattress lifts, he is not surprised. He listens as she bumps through the room.

And then, soft steps in the hall.

The apartment door opening, clicking shut.

That is different.

She comes home at quarter after three.

Why do this to him now? Why tonight, of all nights?

Yesterday Detective Morton called as Carol and Drew were finishing dinner. Ben was out somewhere, having dinner with friends. Both Drew and Carol were trying not to be anxious, to let Ben be a teenager—he's a good kid, after all, never one to give them trouble, not like his sister—but with the one-year anniversary of Jennifer's disappearance fast approaching, the tension pulled tight, unmentioned, as they poked at the Chinese takeout Drew had picked up on the way home from work. Drew asked Carol about her day, her appointment with Dr. Rubin, and she lied, saying that she'd gone, it had been okay, they were still working through her attachment issues. She always lied; Drew had figured that out months ago, but the effort of accusing felt too burdensome, their marriage too fragile to take on more weight. He asked anyway, thinking that soon they might turn a corner and she might decide to start telling the truth.

His cell phone rang as Carol picked up their plates, her food untouched. She glanced at the screen before he did and raised her eyebrows. "The vigil," he said, and Carol nodded, dumping the food in the trash. Ben would have been angry; they had become wasteful people. Later, when Ben got home, he carried his leftovers with him, tinfoil containers of Indian food, which Drew picked at, the refrigerator door hanging open, before going to bed.

The vigil is scheduled for next Saturday—a week after the anniversary but the soonest they could secure a permit. A small affair in a nondescript concrete park on the Lower East Side, near Jennifer's old apartment, just like they'd held at one week and at six months. Candles and flyers. A few TV crews. Another plea for answers.

Detective Morton hadn't called in months. Drew was the one who phoned. Morton was the one who told him there was no news, they'd call when—if—there was. Last week he had left her a voice mail, telling her about the vigil, asking her to come. That must be why she was calling now, but Drew's hand still shook, it always shook, as he answered.

"Hello, Detective. How are you?"

"Mr. Bauer."

Drew liked Morton, her bluntness, her efficiency, her refusal to call him anything but Mr. Bauer. She had always struck him as a woman who got things done, and because of this, he had placed his trust in her, believed everything he'd been told, much to Carol's frustration. But Carol wouldn't make the calls.

"Sorry to be phoning late," Morton said.

Leaning against the sink, Carol folded her arms.

"It's no problem." Drew fiddled with his chopsticks, avoiding his wife's prying look. "What can I do for you, Detective?"

There was a long pause. Drew put the chopsticks down.

"A body's been recovered," Morton said, "in Pennsylvania."

Another body. There had been five, but it had been six months, at least, since the last.

"There are physical similarities," she went on, "to several of our cases. We're bringing it here."

It.

"When?" Drew said.

"Tomorrow. I wanted to give you a heads-up. We'll let you know more when we know more."

Over the past year, he had learned to be patient, gracious.

"Thank you, Detective," he said.

When he hung up, Carol grabbed the phone.

"What?" she said, staring at the screen, as if she'd find the answer spelled out there.

"A lead," Drew said, trying to soften the blow. But she looked at him too intently; he couldn't keep it from her. "Another body."

"It's not her." She dropped the phone on the table, dangerously close to his glass of water. "It's never her."

She was right, of course; it never had been, but every time, the possibility hovered over Drew—the hope, the fear. His daughter coming close, being stolen away again.

Carol picked up a sponge and pressed it against the counter without wiping. "Don't tell Ben," she said, and Drew nodded even though her back was to him. There was no point upsetting Ben unnecessarily.

When his alarm goes off at six, Drew stands over the lump that is his wife and pushes back the impulse to grab her and make her tell him where she went. Instead he goes into the kitchen and starts the coffee. For as long as he can remember, this has been his Friday morning routine: a glass of water while the coffee brews, forty minutes on the treadmill at the gym down the block, back home for a shower, raisin bran with skim milk and a banana for breakfast. He isn't about to change it.

By seven thirty, he has exercised, washed, and fed himself, dressed except for his jacket. He flips his tie over his shoulder as he brushes his teeth. Carol used to come in now, sleepily, and splash her face with water. She'd smile at him, and in her wrinkled nightgown, she'd look cute, her unmade-up face rounder, more youthful, like the girl he met and married. The girl who didn't have to try. She'd stand on her toes and kiss him, the mint of his mouth mixing with the morning dryness of hers.

He spits and licks his lips, imagining their tongues touching. He tries to hold on, but his agitation seeps in until the memory collapses, replaced by the feel of the mattress lifting in the middle of the night, the emptiness at his back.

The alarm clock lights burn 7:47. Late. He'll have to run down the stairs instead of risking the elevator taking too long. He'll arrive at the subway platform sweaty, out of breath. By the time he gets to the morning meeting, his nerves will be fried.

"Carol."

Cupped in his hand, her shoulder feels small, like a child's. Her fragility makes him pause, until she shrugs him off.

"Carol," he says in his normal tone. He says her name louder.

She groans and rolls onto her back, her arm thrown across her face.

"I'm going," he says.

"What?" She peeks out from beneath her elbow. "Okay."

He can smell the booze.

Drew's knees give. He drops onto the edge of the bed. Carol shifts away but after a moment struggles up until she sits against the headboard.

"I'm a little under the weather," she says, not meeting his eye, coughing into her fist.

He presses his hand to her forehead. He has never done this before, although he has watched her do it countless times, with Jennifer, with Ben. She does feel warm, but that could be from the duvet, too much cover for this time of year.

She closes her eyes, and he lingers, taking her warmth into his cool palm.

There is nowhere to go on the Upper West Side at that time of night. She would have had to hail a cab. Imagining her riding away from him, he removes his hand.

"I need more sleep," she says, eyes still closed.

"Carol." He doesn't know what he wants to say, what he is prepared to know.

"Sweetie, don't you have to go?"

He watches the small bones of her neck move as she swallows. She coughs again and lies down, pulling the sheet over her head.

On his way down the hall, he swings open the door to Ben's room, expecting the reassuring sight of his son sound asleep, as Drew would have been at fifteen, in the final days of spring break. But the bed is neatly made, the room empty.

Ben, too.

His son is gone. Drew steps into the room, scanning for a note. Ben, conscientious Ben, would leave one.

"Dad."

In the doorway Ben stands in a T-shirt and baggy shorts, his dusty hair sticking up, chewing on the last fourth of a bagel. A cream cheese smear across his upper lip.

"Aren't you late?" Ben says.

Maybe Drew should just stay home today. Make sure Carol goes to her therapist appointment. Do something with Ben. He stares at his son, trying to remember what his boy likes to do. The walls of Ben's room are bare except for a printout of the periodic table above his desk. The surface of the desk is painfully neat, his laptop closed, textbooks stacked, pencils in the old jelly jar he uses as a holder. Drew resists the urge to knock the jar over, spill the pencils across the floor. Ben would just stand there, chewing his bagel. "What's wrong, Dad?" he'd say, cocking his head, staring with those big brown eyes—Carol's eyes—full of genuine concern.

What isn't wrong?

Drew tries out a laugh. "It's just one of those days," he says.

"What days?"

Drew feels heat rising to his face. Ben finishes his bagel and takes a tissue from his pocket, wipes his hands.

"No meeting this morning," Drew lies.

Ben doesn't step back as he nears, forcing Drew to press into the doorframe as he squeezes past his youngest child.

"Wipe your lip," Drew says and immediately regrets it, that critical tone, but he's already hurrying down the hall, leaving his son behind.

He takes a cab. The driver is listening to a jaunty song in Arabic, synthesizers and caterwauling voices. Any other day, Drew would enjoy the beat, but now he craves nothing more than silence.

He leans forward. "Hey, friend," he says, "mind if we turn that off?"

The driver gives Drew a scathing look in the rearview mirror and switches off the radio. Drew takes out his phone and checks his e-mail, debating whether to send Nancy a message saying he'll be late, to do her best to cover for him. He can't bear the thought of sitting through the morning meeting, acting as if everything is normal.

Screw it.

He types a new message.

```
Nance,

Not going to make it in today.
```

"Friend," he says, leaning forward again, wrinkling his suit jacket, "I've got a change of destination."

Three

Ben, fifteen years old and feeling the apartment's quiet heaviness bearing down on him, doesn't want to wake his mom, but he needs to look at her. He stays at the foot of her bed, the door only a few feet away and cracked open enough for him to make his escape. By now his mom should be in the kitchen, singing along to the radio, on her second cup of coffee. The apartment should smell like toasting bagels, peeled oranges, the humid soapiness of showers. The blinds should be open, the lights on, and his mom should be grinning, saying to him, "It's about time we got this day started."

He tries to remember the last time she said that and can't. The change happened slowly, the mornings growing later, darker, his mom further and further away. He puts this observation in the back of his mind with the others, a catalogue of the ways his family is falling apart. Being an observer is his thing—it puts him at a remove, fortifies him, so that he can stand here watching his mom, listening to her sighs as if she is not who she used to be.

Today he will buy a lock for his room and figure out how to install it.

His mom knocks the covers off her foot. Her toes curl and kick against the air. She lifts her head.

"Why aren't you at school?" she asks, her voice grainy.

"Clear your throat."

She does as he tells her to—he is getting used to this, their reversal of roles—and tries again. Her voice is the same as before. Ben gives up.

"Spring break," he says.

"Right." She moves her jaw up and down, from side to side. "What have you got planned?"

"I'm hanging out with Mike," he says, even though he and Mike haven't been friends since the start of the school year. It was Ben's choice, to become the silent kid. There just didn't seem to be enough words to say what he needed to in order to explain himself, enough space to breathe with the effort of talking. As an unintended consequence, a few girls have developed crushes on him. He pretends not to notice the girls' stares in the hallway, their whispers, the whispers of others. *Use it,* Mike would tell him, but Ben isn't interested in those girls. Eventually, he would have to talk to them, and he'd have nothing to say that they would understand.

His mom lies back down.

Ben goes into the bathroom, fills a glass with water, and sets it and two aspirin on the nightstand beside the alarm clock.

Standing in the doorway, he tries to see his room through his dad's eyes. There is nothing to find offensive, he has made sure of that. After Jennifer moved out, without her permission—without even asking her—his parents emptied her bedroom. They sold her bed and desk on Craigslist, took down the Patti Smith and Diane Arbus posters, and repainted the white walls even whiter. They gathered the photographs of Jennifer and her friends in their cheap plastic frames, the dusty silk flowers stuck in a glass bottle shaped like the Eiffel Tower, the seashells

Jennifer had collected from the beach in Jamaica on the family vacation he barely remembers, and packed them away in a cardboard box, *Jennifer's Keepsakes* written on the sides and top by his mom in black marker. They shoved the floral sheets and comforter into garbage bags, along with the clothes still left in the closet, and carted them off to Housing Works. Finally they tore up the pale-pink carpet, stained by spilled juice and snuck wine, the soles of Jennifer's boots, what looked like drops of blood, and paid men to sand and finish the hardwood floor. For a week the room stood empty, all traces of Jennifer erased.

When Jennifer came over for dinner that Sunday, she stood in the middle of the room and screamed, her voice echoing off the bare walls. Only Ben knew she was mostly kidding, making a scene for their shared amusement, riling up their mom the way she liked to.

"You weren't using it, sweetie," their mom said from the doorway, a wineglass clutched between her hands. Their dad stayed at the dining room table. By the time they returned, he had finished his meal and was reading the *Wall Street Journal*.

Their mom put her arm around Jennifer. "We didn't think you'd mind," she said. Over her shoulder, Jennifer stuck out her front teeth and rolled her eyes at Ben.

"Once you're gone," Jennifer said, "you're gone."

"Outta here," he said.

"Good riddance."

"Kids, please."

"It's okay," Jennifer said, heading toward the door. "I never liked it here anyway. You wouldn't let me paint the walls."

"Red," their mom said. "Like a brothel."

"Red!" shouted Jennifer from the hallway. "With black trim!"

Their mom turned in a slow circle, the wineglass pressed to her lips, as if reconsidering.

Jennifer didn't come to dinner the next Sunday or the one after that. She stayed away until their mom bribed her with cash. Jennifer showed Ben the five twenties, folded over each other, which their mom had palmed to her as she came through the door, as if conducting a drug deal.

"Watch and learn," she said, but Ben could never pull it off. Jennifer understood how to push their parents' boundaries just far enough for them to bend. Ben worried that if he pushed, the boundaries would cave and he'd find himself alone on the other side.

Which is where he is now, alone on the other side. Although he isn't sure which side is which, who has left whom behind.

His parents turned Jennifer's room into an office. They moved in a desk purchased at an antique store called Olde Good Things. The desk is old, but Ben sees nothing good about it. Big and hulking, it is a desk in his dad's style, meant for his mom and the interior design business she's always talking about launching. In two years, Ben has never seen his mom sit at that desk. It has become the place in the apartment where things accumulate in piles: unopened mail, never-read magazines, Christmas decorations, clothing that needs to be altered or repaired.

And Jennifer's files. Ben has thought about searching through the clutter and finding the manila folders. He has never seen them, but he knows of their existence. On TV there are always files on missing persons, ongoing investigations. Someone like who his mom used to be would demand copies of her own. Where her children were concerned, she knew no fear.

He steps into the room, but as always, the enormity of the mess on the desk makes him change his mind and step back out.

That Sunday Jennifer had slipped one of the twenties into the back pocket of his jeans as she hugged him good-bye. He wishes he could remember what he spent it on. Something stupid. Comic books or lunches at McDonald's or some movie Mike wanted to see and Ben forgot about the moment they left the theater. If he had that twenty now, he would save it. He'd put it in the envelope tucked beneath his mattress, along with the money he's saved from Christmas and his birthday, the fives he's taken here and there from his mom's wallet. Every night he'd fall asleep knowing Jennifer's twenty was there, secure for when the world stopped working.

Jennifer used to worry about him—what a good boy he was, a people-pleaser. "You've got to live your own life," she told him, "not everyone else's."

He has been foolish; he should have gotten a lock for his room a long time ago. If his dad finds the money, if he finds any clue of the life Ben is creating for himself, he'll freak out; he'll never understand.

For weeks after Jennifer moved out, she called Ben every night. He'd lie under his covers and tell her about his day, what happened at school, and she'd give him advice: how to deal with Mike and Aiden fighting without getting stuck in the middle, whether or not Marissa in honors math was flirting with him, which teachers' classes he really should study for and which could be blown off. She'd tell him about the photographs she'd taken, about her friend Sandra and the club they'd gone to the night before. She'd make him laugh, exaggerating their mishaps and bravado. Theirs was a different city, full of adult wonder and adventure. He longed to be part of it, but it frightened him a little, too, and he was happy to be in his warm, safe bed, listening to her stories with his parents asleep down the hall.

At home everything went on as it always did, except that without Jennifer, the days were more boring. Ben's mom clung a little tighter, asking a lot of questions but seeming distracted when he answered, buying him little presents—candy bars, a skateboard magazine, new headphones—and leaving them on his bed. His dad barely seemed to notice him, except at dinner or on the weekend, when his dad would suddenly look up from his food or iPad or away from the TV and stare at Ben, a puzzled expression on his face. "How's school?" he'd say, and Ben would tell him it was fine. "Good," his dad would say. And then, "Tell me if you need any help on your math homework." Or "We'll have to go to the museum one of these days, see that *T. rex*," something they had done once or twice when Ben was little.

"Sure," Ben would say, and his dad would smile, relieved of his duties, and go back to what he'd been doing.

Ben visited Jennifer at her apartment a couple of times, but its stark reality was a disturbing contrast to the glamour he'd envisioned when they'd talked on the phone. She seemed uncomfortable, too, perched on the edge of the mattress that took up her entire bedroom, her knees folded into her chest. She had started collecting saint candles—ironically, she said, at first, and because they were cheap, an easy way to make a room interesting, but she fell in love with their beauty, the stories they could tell—and the impassive faces of saints stared at him from the windowsill, the perimeter of the floor. Jennifer preferred to meet him at a restaurant outside of the neighborhood or to come uptown if he had the place to himself.

When their parents were home, they demanded too much, their mom bombarding Jennifer with questions, her eyes shining with need, their father a hulking presence, delivering pointed digs at Jennifer for dropping out of college. When their parents were out, the apartment exhaled. Ben and Jennifer together had always felt natural, safe, as if they were each other's real family, their mom and dad intruders.

As children, Jennifer and Ben used to make forts, throwing a bedsheet across the back of the couch, crawling under the dining room table. They would watch their parents' feet pad across the carpet and would whisper to each other, or not say anything, just revel in the feeling of being hidden, of owning a space of their own. Jennifer, six years older, played these games long after she'd outgrown them. Ben misses those days, how close she was, how present, how he could rely on her to always reach out a hand and pull him in after her.

Over time her visits home became less and less frequent. "When am I going to see you?" he'd say, and she'd laugh and tell him, "Soon, soon" and launch into a story about the weekend, losing her shoe on the dance floor or spending the night in Tompkins Square Park, taking pictures, and walking along Avenue A as the sun came up.

That October Hurricane Sandy hit. In the days leading up to it, as the forecast worsened, Ben's mom told Jennifer to come back home. The Upper West Side hills would be safe from flooding; downtown, Jennifer would be at risk. But of course Jennifer stayed. Ben understood: she was having too much fun to leave. She belonged there now, and he envied her that freedom, a life of her own making.

Ben and his parents slept through the storm and wandered out the next morning to puddles, branches in the street. The coffee shops and bodegas were opening; his dad took a cab to his office in Midtown. But they couldn't reach Jennifer. His mom had the TV on in the living room, the radio in the kitchen, the voices of the newscasters merging to nonsense as they described the flooding. In his room, Ben called Jennifer, thinking she would answer if she saw his name on the screen. But every time the call went to voice mail.

She resurfaced that evening, letting herself in as they were finishing dinner. "My phone died," she said, looking a little guilty. She stayed long enough to eat and recharge her phone and then she was off again, swallowed up by the darkness. After that, she called Ben only occasionally, usually late at night, her voice tired and slurred. He left his phone by his pillow, just in case.

Ben was a baby on 9/11, but he has done his own research, beyond what he's been taught at school: he's seen the pictures, read the transcripts of last phone calls, listened to the names intoned on TV on every anniversary. He's been raised with the awareness that in an instant, everything can be taken from you, but he didn't believe it for himself until Hurricane Sandy, when Jennifer wasn't answering her phone and he couldn't escape the thought that the flood had swept her up, pulled her under. He saw his mom's damp eyes, his dad's clenched jaw, as they told each other, over and over, that her phone must have died, she was without power, she'd get in touch soon. And even though that turned out to be true, the possibility of loss shimmered there, a premonition.

And then Jennifer was gone, for real. When they'd all stopped worrying. When they were just going about their lives, taking everything for granted.

Ben doesn't want to be caught unawares again. There's a whole system to preparation, a whole society, he has discovered, devoted to it. The more he read online, the more he began to believe in the evidence; the science is there. The end of the world is coming, whether by an act of man or an act of God—it makes no difference; at this point they are one and the same. And when the End does come, he will be ready to face it. He won't allow the people he loves most to be vulnerable. He will do what he can to protect them; he will lead them to safety.

He leaves a note for his mom on the refrigerator door, attached by a rectangular magnet from one of his dad's business things. The note is only a gesture. His mom won't need him. She thinks she can take care of herself.

"Aren't you on spring break?" Rob asks as Ben comes through the lobby.

Rob is Ben's favorite doorman. The day they found out Jennifer was missing, Rob cried openly, his head drooped and his big shoulders shaking. Ben imagines that in another life, Rob and Jennifer would be married, living in an apartment a few blocks over, Jennifer making her art, Rob doing well in his classes at John Jay. Ben would go over there after school and play the video games his dad doesn't allow. He'd have his own key, and they would keep his favorite snacks—Doritos, Dr Pepper, those grainy fig bars from the bodega down the street—on hand.

"Seize the day," Ben says, and Rob laughs.

"Smart kid," Rob says. "You're going to take over the world."

Ben returns Rob's smile, but if there is anything he's learned in the past year, it's the fact of his own insignificance. He's done believing he can conquer the world. Now he's just biding his time until he has to confront it.

The sun sparkles the sidewalk. He puts his skateboard down and pushes off, the breeze ruffling the hair on the back of his neck. At the corner he heads south.

Four

In another life Drew would have been a deep-sea fisherman, spending weeks on the water alone. As a child he begged his parents to take him to see the boats, which meant coming here, to Battery Park, where he would sit on a bench between his father and mother while they passed a soft pretzel back and forth above his head, salt scattering across his knees. After half an hour, they would have had enough. His mother would want to go shopping. His father would be impatient to get back to their house in Queens, where he could crack open a beer and watch whatever game was on and forget about Manhattan, where he had to come every weekday in a loathed suit and tie, and shoes that pinched his wide feet. But half an hour was never enough for Drew. He'd have just gotten into his daydream, his parents' voices receding along with the car horns and hawkers' shouts, the sound of the waves pulsating in his ears, becoming the natural rhythm of his blood.

New York City consists of islands, a fact Drew likes to make himself stop and consider, a fact he wonders at. The best city in the world, surrounded on all sides by water: fragile, imperishable, resilient. In another life Drew would be stronger. He would have sea legs, solid as steel.

The day is already warming up. He takes off his suit jacket, lays it across the back of the bench, rolls up his sleeves. The breeze feels good on his bare arms, and he tilts his chin up toward the sun.

When he was in high school, he and his buddies would skip class— just once in a while, never enough to affect their grades or get their parents called—and take the subway to Times Square. They'd eat greasy pizza and push each other in front of the sex shops, none of them brave enough to go inside. But now—what? He hates Times Square, the herds of tourists. And it's too early for pizza.

The coffee he bought from the cart on the corner is lukewarm, too strong. He doesn't need it anyway. He's jittery, the morning resonating through his nerves. Without deciding to, he reaches into the inside pocket of his jacket and removes the notebook he has been carrying for the past year, since Jennifer went missing. In Duane Reade he'd felt big and cumbersome standing in front of the school supplies, all those little bottles of glue and safety scissors in primary colors. This notebook cost seventy-nine cents and has a navy-blue cover, which has become scratched, although he doesn't know how. He takes the notebook out of his pocket only to write in it or change from one jacket to another. He never leaves it out for someone to discover, or for him to lose. The notebook is his gift to Jennifer, his promise that she will be found, that someday he will have the chance to give it to her and try to explain himself. He doesn't want to forget anything.

Like that late-fall day when Jennifer was four. Before Ben. Something was wrong with Carol. The flu, or "a case of the blues," as she called it. She asked Drew to take Jennifer out for the day, and he brought her here to see the boats. She was enthusiastic at first, looking where he pointed, echoing the names. Sailboat. Tugboat. Ferry. Tanker. But soon he felt her excitement wane. She leaned into him, her body growing heavier against his side, until she fell asleep. He hesitated, unsure what to do, worried and slightly angry that he had bored her. He was tempted to nudge her awake. Right then a cruise ship passed, monstrous in size, passengers waving from the decks. "Look, pumpkinseed," he said, and in her sleep, she clutched the fabric of his sleeve.

He writes it all down.

> *The sun made the wisps of hair around your face almost invisible. Your mouth puckered, like you tasted something sour in your dream. I asked you later, and you told me Sour Patch Kids, so I bought a bag at a bodega on the way home. We shared it in secret walking back from the subway. You held my hand and jumped over the cracks in the sidewalk. When we came to an especially big crack, you would say, "One, two, three, jump," and I would lift you by the arm, dangling you above the pavement, up and over. We cheered like some great feat had been accomplished.*

The sweet memories, yes, but he is a realist—he has to remember the bitter ones, too. As a teenager she would narrow her eyes when he spoke to her, or close her eyes completely, lolling her head on the couch as if he had put her to sleep. She would tell him she didn't care, so one day he said it right back to her, enunciating each word slowly. "I. Don't. Care." And that night, instead of coming home late, she didn't come home at all. Drew found Carol the next morning in the kitchen, her hands shaking from all the coffee she had drunk. She wouldn't speak to him. When Jennifer finally came back that afternoon, offering no apologies and no excuses, Carol took her hand and led her to her bedroom, shutting the door behind them.

He must go back there, force himself to be closed out again, staring at her bedroom door, at the wooden sign they'd bought at an art festival when Jennifer was little, her name written in curling vines, pink roses sprouting.

Were you talking about me?

Writing it feels pathetic, but every question, every detail, carries weight now, too important to let go. He flips through the notebook. It is almost full, and he still isn't any closer to understanding what is happening to his family.

He turns to a new page.

Who is Carol fucking?

That word, *fucking*—he has never liked it. He can't decide if he believes it or not. He crosses out the sentence, pressing so hard the pen bleeds into the page.

In the chest pocket of his shirt, his phone vibrates. He places his hand over it. Either Morton or work. Or Carol. He doesn't want to talk to any of them.

He answers without looking at the screen.

"Mr. Bauer."

"Yes, Detective. Hello."

A low whistle on the water, the Staten Island Ferry's launch.

"Your daughter had a tattoo," Morton says, straight to business, as usual.

It's not a question, but Drew answers anyway. "That's what I've been told."

"On her wrist. A Celtic knot."

"Yes." Drew closes the notebook, rubs the cover with the heel of his hand. He never saw the tattoo himself, just the approximation Carol drew on a piece of graph paper for the police.

"There's a match," Morton says.

His hand stills. On the water, the ferry seems to stop.

"The body is expected this afternoon. We'd like you to come down."

"Down?" Drew says.

"To the medical examiner's office. For identification."

He's never been called down before. Always there's been a differ-ence, a saving grace. There could be yet, he tells himself. The tattoo wasn't an original design. How many other women Jennifer's age have that tattoo, or something similar?

Nothing is certain. The body isn't even in the city.

"We'll let you know when," Morton says.

He thanks her—*Always be gracious*—and puts his phone back in his shirt pocket.

As the ferry passes the Statue of Liberty, he thinks that he should feel something, some twinge in his chest, some twist in his stomach, telling him if the body is Jennifer's. But he doesn't. He feels nothing.

His hands are covered in ink.

He puts on his suit jacket, tucking the notebook where it always goes, into the left inside pocket.

Five

Ben waits on Sandra's stoop, his skateboard balanced between his knees, his chin resting on top. The street looks abandoned. The bars will not lift their metal shutters for hours, the office workers have already left for the day, the kids, off school, are still asleep. So are the artists. He had to ring the buzzer twice and heard the blurriness in Sandra's voice, although when she realized who it was, she tried to hide it. A few months ago she might have fooled him, but he knows her too well now. He spins the wheels on his skateboard. Sandra has become his friend.

The door creaks, and he turns to see Sandra stepping out in a green kimono, her dark hair gathered up in a messy bun. Her feet are bare, her purple toenail polish chipped. She nudges him with her foot, and he scoots over, giving her room on the step.

Her skin is warm. She smells good, like rumpled sheets and the sandalwood incense she burns.

"God," she says and shields her eyes with her hand even though the sun has gone behind the clouds. He likes the color of her kimono; it matches her eyes. He considers telling her this. Instead he concentrates on the way the silk has worn thin on the wide bell sleeve. Soon there will be holes.

She sighs and takes out a pack of cigarettes, offers one to Ben. Together they smoke and watch the street.

"This is what it'll look like at the End," Ben says, "except the streets will be rivers."

Sandra gives the grunt that is her version of a laugh—*she* gets him.

He recognizes the dark circles beneath her eyes from his mom: Sandra didn't take her makeup off last night. She might have returned only a few hours ago, living while he slept.

"You want to hear something funny?" she says, her voice hoarse as if she spent the night shouting. "Trey's going to do an exhibit."

Ben doesn't know who Trey is.

"You mean your collages?" he asks.

Sandra nods, still looking across the street, up at a second-floor window. Ben looks, too, and sees nothing—maybe a movement in the curtain.

"Who's Trey?" Ben says.

Flicking ash into the street, Sandra breaks into a grin. "You're jealous."

Ben feels himself blush. He grips his skateboard and tries to fight it.

"Kidding." Sandra bumps her shoulder against his. "Trey's the way in." She looks straight at Ben for the first time that morning, and her tongue pokes out between her teeth in the way that makes his heart double in size. "Owner's son," she says.

"What's he look like?"

"Come off it, kid."

"I just want to know him," Ben says, "if I see him."

Sandra leans back on her elbows, and Ben notices that the worn-away spots on her sleeve match where the fabric meets the concrete.

"Tall," she says, squinting as if watching Trey from a distance, trying to make him out. "Skinny. Like skeletal skinny. Heroin skinny. Bad skin. Awesome tattoo of a dragon wrapping up his neck. Eyebrow piercings. Likes denim and leather. Great smile. Dazzling teeth. If you see an ugly dude with a movie-star smile wearing old-school East Village chic, that's Trey."

"Did my sister know him?"

"You bet. They dated for a while."

Ben allows this information to settle: his beautiful sister having sex with an ugly dude with a movie-star smile. It would have been the movie-star smile that got her. Or his parents with the art gallery.

"Before you ask," Sandra says. "The police questioned him."

Ben wasn't going to ask.

"They were that close?"

"Kid, the police talked to everyone. And no, I wouldn't call them particularly close. They dated for, like, three weeks a couple years ago. *Dated* isn't even the right word."

"What is the right word?"

Sandra raises her eyebrows. Ben knows. He just wants to make her say it.

"Use your imagination," she says.

"I want to meet him."

She presses down on Ben's shoulder, propelling herself upward, and stretches both arms above her head. She points the toes of one foot, then the other, like the ballet dancer she used to be when she was Ben's age.

"I could use coffee," she says. "Best cup's at the diner on Houston. You got cash on you?"

As she starts down the steps, Ben glances up at her window, realizing someone, probably Trey, is inside.

The air in the diner hangs, humid with eggs and coffee, noisy with the clatter of silverware and the radio playing eighties pop. Men in work boots line the counter; in the corner by the window two young women sit with their knees touching and heads bent close together, waffles congealing on their plates. No one seems to be talking except the waitresses, who yell back and forth to the guys in the kitchen. The guys answer in Spanish and make the waitresses laugh.

No one gives Sandra's kimono or bare feet a second look. She swoops into a booth at the back as if it has been waiting, reserved, for her arrival. The brown plastic of the seats is cracked, the Formica table sticky with syrup. Sandra orders two coffees and asks the waitress for a glass of water. She pours the water on a napkin, wipes the table. "Better?" she says.

The coffee burns Ben's tongue. He drinks it black, the way Sandra drinks it, the way Jennifer drank it. The taste is growing on him, although he still can't say he likes it. Yet every time he drinks it, he feels stronger. Like the observations he keeps secret, the coffee fortifies him.

Sandra flips through the menu. "Pancakes," she says.

The photographs beside the descriptions—some of the colors muted, others too bright—make Ben's stomach turn.

"He'll share with me," Sandra tells the waitress. "Extra whipped cream, please. And strawberries."

Ben thinks about Trey in Sandra's bed, beneath the quilt that Sandra's mother made. Sandra wrapped that quilt around Ben the first afternoon he showed up at her apartment. The squares are cut from clothes Sandra wore as a child. Her favorite play outfits next to dresses for holidays, the first day of school, and dance recitals. Red velvet. Blue-and-green striped cotton. Yellow satin. Pink corduroy. The quilt smells like sandalwood and soap. It feels like a second skin.

Trey will ruin it.

Ben takes a big gulp of coffee. The waitress appears with the pot and refills his cup.

"The exhibit," he says.

"What?" Sandra has been staring off into space, or at the men at the counter. Ben looks at them, but they hunch over their eggs, consumed by the job at hand.

"Oh, yeah." Her bun has almost come loose, and she takes it down, shakes out her hair. "I'm going to have him put up some of Jen's photos, too."

"Which ones?"

"Want to help me choose?"

The offer surprises Ben. "Yeah," he says. "Sure."

"Come over later. We'll spread everything out. You can choose something for yourself, too. I've been a hoarder."

"That's okay," Ben says. "She's safe with you."

Sandra touches his hand. "Thank you for saying that."

"I mean it. My parents wouldn't know what to do with her photographs. They got rid of all her stuff." He sees Sandra's expression harden and stops, reverses. "A long time ago. Before this. But that's not the point. The point is they didn't know her. They didn't care."

"I won't take sides," Sandra says and puts her spoon in her coffee, stirs, even though she has put nothing in it. She takes out the spoon, licks it, sets it back on the table. "Do your parents know where you are?"

Ben laughs.

"Whose fault is that?" Sandra says.

"Why would I tell them?"

"Exactly. Don't you think Jen felt the same way?"

Ben slouches. He doesn't like when Sandra gets like this; he didn't come for a lecture.

"I'm just saying don't be too hard on them," she says. "Your mom especially. She's a pretty good mom, all things considered."

"You didn't see her this morning."

"We're all entitled to a bad morning," Sandra says.

The mound of whipped cream trembles as the waitress places the pancakes on the table. The red of the strawberries looks artificial. *Frozen,* Ben thinks, although he doesn't know why.

Sandra picks up a fork and pushes the plate toward him. "They're as big as my head," she says.

He watches her eat. She closes her eyes.

"So good," she says around a mouthful. She cuts through all three layers and holds out her fork to Ben. He leans forward, opens his mouth wide. He feels the whipped cream on his lips. He can barely chew so much food, but he has to agree—the pancakes are the best he's ever had.

They eat in silence until all that is left is a pool of red, swirled with white.

Sandra throws down her fork. Ben feels sick. His mouth tastes sour with coffee. The waitress comes back with the pot, but Sandra doesn't wave her away so neither does he. There is no hurry in this place, no need to face the future. He can see why Sandra likes it. You could stay here forever, drinking cup after cup of coffee, allowing the black liquid to fill your veins, fill you up, forgetting that there was ever anything else.

The men in work boots have left, replaced by an old, bent-backed couple spooning oatmeal into their mouths. The husband wears a fedora, the wife a threadbare cardigan. Their canes lean together in the space between their stools.

Ben thinks again of Trey in Sandra's bed. If you loved someone, you wouldn't call him "an ugly dude," even if you added "with a movie-star smile."

Sandra pushes her hair behind her ears. When Ben first met her, he found her appearance confusing, intimidating. She is small, barely coming up to his shoulder, and bony, but her arms and legs have hard muscle. Her upturned nose looks like the ones on the cute, popular girls at school, but she wears a silver ring through its septum. Silver studs dot each earlobe, and she talks about getting surface piercings along her collarbone. They would look amazing; he has fantasized about running his tongue across their cool surfaces, a contrast to the heat of her skin.

On her wrist is a tattoo, a Celtic friendship knot. Jennifer got the same one. They went to the tattoo parlor together, lay down side by side. Through the process, they held hands.

Ben stares down at his own blank wrists.

"I want a tattoo," he says. "For Jen."

"Think about it," Sandra says.

"I have."

"Do me a favor? Sit on the idea a few more weeks, and if you still want it, I'll take you."

"Do you regret yours?"

"No. But I wasn't fifteen." Beneath the table she presses her legs against his, kicking until she has the skateboard under her feet. She grins, although he didn't put up a fight.

"How old were you when you got your first piercing?"

"Fourteen. But piercings you can take out. I don't even have that one anymore."

Ben wonders where it was.

"I'm just doing my duty," she says. "You've become mine to look after."

Mine.

He is pretty sure she has never used that word to describe Trey.

Six

There was a hand on her elbow, guiding her out of the club. A chill in the air, dampness. Carol shivered. Her heel caught in the sidewalk. She had the sense that she was falling, and an arm was around her shoulders, righting her. The intrusion angered her. She may have said, "Let me fall." She may have said, "Get off me." But she doubts it. The overwhelming feeling was one of compliance. A child being put back into bed, where she belonged.

And she woke up here, with Drew snoring beside her. Somehow she had remembered to undress, push the clothes into the bottom of the hamper, slip a nightgown over her head. She had not brushed her hair, and she reaches up now, tugs her fingers through the tangles.

That damn light around the window.

She presses her palms against her stomach, liking the hollow forming, the sharp jut of hip bones. The way they hurt when she lies on her stomach. *What diet are you on?* she imagines the mothers asking at PTO. *Are you doing SoulCycle? Boot camp? Bikram? No,* she'd say. *It's the Missing Daughter Cleanse. You should try it.*

Oh, she's becoming a wicked woman.

In the bathroom she takes off her nightgown before turning on the overhead light. Under its blinding glare, the woman in the mirror isn't as terrible as Carol expected. Yes, her hair is greasy and knotted, her skin washed-out, her lips chapped. Dark circles make her eyes look bruised. But her eyes do not glow an angry red. No vomit clings to her chin. Her teeth are not fanged. She has not turned into a wraith, not yet.

As she turns on the shower, she grows dizzy at the memory of Drew's hand on her forehead, searching for the fever that wasn't there.

He hasn't touched her intimately in months, not since the last time Morton called about a body. She let him then because she understood he needed her. She needed him, too, but not for sex. Her body closed up, a fist beneath him. He pressed into her anyway. He hadn't noticed, and she hadn't stopped him. She could do it that way once, and never again.

Lying next to him, she often finds herself staring at the mole between his shoulder blades, thinking, *I hate you, hate you, hate you.* Then she switches. *I love you, love you, love you.*

I hate you. I love you. Someday the wrong word will slip out, at the wrong time.

She knows the body is not Jennifer's.

Last night Carol got no closer to her daughter, but a man young enough to be Carol's child bought her a drink. They sat at one of the little tables, the candlelight turning their faces into angles and shadows. He reached over and fingered the crosses dangling from her ears. He pulled slightly. Her ear burned. She shook her head, brushing his hand away.

A sloppy drinker, he spilled wine onto the table, onto the cuffs of his shirt. Jennifer would not have been impressed. Whoever took her would have had to seduce her, convince her. She didn't give of herself easily.

But the young man kept buying Carol drinks, and the club stayed empty.

"Let's dance," he said.

Carol considered for only a second. She couldn't stand the thought of this silly, sloppy man's arms around her, his squat hands pressing into her hips. She had been a good dancer at one point in her life.

He grew bored. She noticed him scanning the room, searching for a better option.

How many drinks? Four, five?

Six.

The room grew closer and suddenly expanded out, disorienting her, wavering space all around, and the features of the man blurred.

The hand on her elbow. The cold, damp air. Goose bumps on her arms.

She remembers a feeling of shame. She had to ask the cabdriver to pull over. She opened the door and vomited into the gutter.

"I'm sorry."

The driver laughed. "At least you warned me," he said, shaking his head. "If you didn't warn me, you'd be walking right now."

She shudders to think of all the things the driver has seen, the spills he has had to clean up. The long shower he must take every morning, cleansing the ugliness of New York off his skin, out of his mind.

She never used to consider such things.

Carol steps under the blast of water before it gets warm. Her hands run up and down her sides. She presses soapy fingers into her rib cage. Just a little more effort, and she could pry the bones apart.

Humiliation creeps up slowly, a prickling along her spine. What was Drew thinking as he sat on the bed, his palm to her forehead, as if she were a child begging off school? How could he not hate her by now?

She scrubs her skin pink, turns off the shower, and listens to the drip of the pipes. Behind the closed bathroom door, she is aware of the empty apartment, the rooms unfurling. The apartment is her domain—she picked it out, decorated it, redecorated it twice. But nothing feels the way it should anymore. Nothing feels like hers.

"Hello," she shouts, her voice bouncing off the tiles. "Hello?"

This is what her days are like; she loses track: Drew goes into the office, Ben goes to school. The same routine as before, but then she had things to do. Plans. Only now she has a hard time remembering what those plans were.

Standing in front of her closet naked, dripping wet, she pushes hangers around, tempted to play dress-up again, recreate the woman who went to Inferno last night. The first time she put on one of Jennifer's T-shirts, she took it off immediately. The smell, the touch of the cotton had been too much. The next time, she wore one of Jennifer's loose sundresses for an hour, walking from room to room, feeling the swish of fabric against her bare legs. Soon she began to do her hair, her makeup, washing her face and changing her clothes before Drew and Ben got home.

Carol's foot knocks against something, and she looks down to see the boots she wore last night, fallen over each other. She wasn't so careful after all. Crouching, she grabs the boots and stuffs them back into their box, pushes the box to the back of the closet. She bought the boots online last week: knee-high, black leather, five-inch heels, like a pair Jennifer used to own. If Drew saw them, he'd think she was having an affair. As far as he knows, she's still the woman who swore off high heels decades ago, who proclaimed that comfort matters most. She of the eco-friendly loafers and ballet flats. The jeans and button-downs. The ankle-length flowing skirts.

She always envied Jennifer's ability to reshape herself into anyone she wanted to be. Even as a little girl, Jennifer excelled at dress-up. She would parade up and down the hall in Carol's old bridesmaid dresses, the hems trailing after her, wearing them with more self-possession— more of a right—than Carol had. "I'm a princess," she'd say, twirling in front of the mirror, and Carol would get down on her knees and smooth out the fabric, a lady-in-waiting.

The last time Carol saw her daughter, she was changing trains at Forty-Second Street when she spotted Jennifer through the crowd. She called out, but Jennifer didn't hear her. As Carol watched Jennifer move away, she became overwhelmed by how beautiful her daughter looked, how much she was her own person, confidently charting her course through the city. Jennifer was wearing a jacket Carol had never seen: light-blue suede, cinched tightly at the waist with a black-and-blue brocade belt. Black boots fit snuggly around her calves, and her blond hair, curlier than Carol had ever seen it, swung around her shoulders. Carol felt a swelling pride that somehow that extraordinary woman had come from her.

While emptying Jennifer's apartment, Carol searched in vain for the jacket. On her first visit to Sandra's, she asked if Sandra knew where it was. Sandra claimed she didn't, but while she was in the bathroom, Carol opened her closet, pushed through the hangers. Her hands came away empty, smelling of sandalwood.

The jacket became her recurring dream. The blue suede grasped by a male hand, fingers long, fingernails clean. Elegant hands that could play the piano, wield a paintbrush, make an incision, remove an organ. Hands that tore the jacket from Jennifer's shoulders. Hands that wrapped around Jennifer's throat.

On a hunch, she called Inferno. Yes, she was told, a blue suede jacket had been found. She sent Sandra to collect it. The belt was missing, but otherwise, it was in perfect condition. Now it hangs in the back of Carol's closet, behind her good dresses in their dry-cleaning bags. She kneels next to the boots in their shoebox and reaches up, touches the jacket's hem, the suede so soft. She sticks her nose in the lining and inhales.

In the kitchen she finds a note on the refrigerator door:

> *See you at dinner*
> *Love,*
> *Ben*

She slips the Post-it into the pocket of her bathrobe and tries to remember the name of Ben's friend. Mike. Is he the chubby kid? The redhead? The one whose parents produce Broadway plays? Is his mother that horrible woman with the Maltese she carries everywhere, tucked beneath her arm? God, that woman's perfume, like she bathes in it.

Mike doesn't strike Carol as the name of a bad kid.

She drinks her coffee while leaning against the counter in front of the sink, staring across the air shaft at the opposite window. Today the blinds are drawn, but sometimes she sees an old woman. Her cat lounges on the sill, and the old woman sits next to it, her hand sliding over its long gray back in even strokes. Thinking about it makes Carol's back twitch. If Ben isn't home by five, she'll call his cell phone. Or send him a text. Maybe she'll send a text right now. *Have fun, sweetie. Be safe.* Or: *Mom misses you.*

The man last night wasn't named Mike, but something similar. One syllable, bland, a male name that transcends generations. Tom or Tim or Dave.

In the opposite window, the blind jerks up. The old woman sets the cat on the sill, where it arches its back and yawns. The old woman disappears, reappears with a cup. She looks out. Carol raises her hand in greeting, but the old woman sips her drink and peers down into the alley. Carol moves closer, presses her hand against the glass. The woman looks up, straight at her, straight through her.

The man's name was Dan.

The telephone rings, making Carol jump and spill coffee down the front of her bathrobe. She grabs a sponge. The phone keeps ringing. It might be Ben. It might be Drew, saying the body is here.

It might be Jennifer.

"Hi," Drew says. "You okay?"

She slides down the counter until she sits on the floor. Her bathrobe falls open, exposing her breasts, and she takes hold of the fabric, pulls it shut, clenches it there.

"Yes," she says.

"You got some rest?"

"Yes."

"Good."

In the background she hears a siren wail.

"Where are you?" she says.

"Heading back to the office. Lunch meeting."

She looks at the clock on the microwave. Twelve forty.

"I heard from Morton," he says. "They want me to come down."

"Where?"

"The morgue, I guess."

"For what?"

He pauses. "To see the body."

"It's not her. You need to tell them that."

"I'm going to have to go down," he says.

"When?"

"I don't know. Do you . . . would you like to come with me?"

"Why? No. Drew, it's not her."

Another siren. They wait as it fades.

"Are you going to see Dr. Rubin?" Drew says. "I think today would be a good day to keep your appointment."

"Yes." She looks at her legs splayed in front of her and can't imagine moving them. "In a bit."

Her husband says something she misses.

"What was that?"

"I can come home, if you need me."

"No. I'm fine."

She holds the receiver away from her ear.

He is saying something else.

"When I find out any—"

"Okay, sweetie," she says.

She puts the phone down. Her appointment with Dr. Rubin is at one. She can make it if she hurries. She'll have to go with wet hair, no makeup, in whatever clothes she finds first. She'll have to hail a cab. She'll have to sit for fifty minutes and talk about things she doesn't want to talk about, feel things she doesn't want to feel. Not in front of a stranger. Not in front of anyone.

The minute number changes. Again and again and again.

She lies down on the floor.

Too late now.

Seven

Although Drew hadn't expected anything different from Carol, he had hoped to be surprised, to be asked back home. To be needed. Now, unaccustomed to empty hours, home an impossibility, he doesn't know what to do with himself.

He checks his phone again—on and fully charged.

Drew does have a lunch meeting, at one o'clock. He decides to go there now and then to the office, where he should have gone to begin with. Idle hands are the devil's workshop, as his mother used to say. Best to keep busy. Best to keep your mind occupied and your emotions in check.

Standing on the subway platform, scrolling through his work e-mail, he can almost pretend it's a normal day. He reads one message after another, retaining nothing.

The train screeches to a halt. Drew puts his phone away and watches the passengers get off. He watches the people waiting get on. He presses his back against the grimy tile and exhales hard, blowing out his cheeks, vibrating his lips. He misses his daughter; he misses his wife. He wants the old Carol back, with her bright, ready smile and habit of absently putting her hand on his thigh while they watch TV. He wants her laugh, mouth open and head thrown back so he can see into her throat. He wants to wake and, without looking, know that she is beside him and his two children are asleep down the hall.

The doors shut. The train pulls out of the station, the wind blowing grit into Drew's eyes. He rubs them with his thumbs, and there, finally, are tears. He readies himself for the onslaught, but when he takes his hands away and blinks, his vision clears.

At the far end of the platform, an old Chinese man with a hunched back plays the violin. Otherwise, Drew is alone. He watches, transfixed, as two rats thread their way over and under the rails, stopping now and again to sniff the air.

Three more trains pass before Drew gets on board. At Grand Central, he doesn't leave the station. Before he has the chance to change his mind, he runs up the stairs and down the other side, and just catches the next 6 train downtown.

He isn't sure he has the right building. He has been here only once before, with Carol, and then he had been following her. They had come with a chocolate cake. A thank-you, although he had never been certain for what.

At the base of the stoop, he reconsiders, but arriving late to the lunch meeting would look worse than not going at all, and he has come all the way down here. He might never have the nerve to come again.

The right name beside the buzzer strikes him as phenomenal for a building in this shape, rent stabilized most certainly, if not rent controlled, but there it is. An omen, like his mother was always looking for. She could find them anywhere: two pigeons on a window ledge, a black cat in a window, a heart-shaped crack in the sidewalk.

He presses the buzzer and waits, peering through the smudged glass panel on the door, making out two brown steps, dusty yellow floor tiles.

The intercom crackles.

"Hello," he says, leaning in, his lips almost touching the metal. "Sandra? Hello?"

"Who is this?"

"Drew."

But his name would mean nothing to her.

"Jennifer's father."

Silence. Even the crackle disappears. Anger replaces his uncertainty—he has come here for his family; he will not be refused. He presses the buzzer again, holding his finger down.

Eight

Ben likes to ride in the first subway car, where he can watch the track swoop toward him through the little window in front. Jennifer taught him how. When they were little, they would beg their parents to go in the first car. Their mom always acquiesced; their dad would, too, unless they were running late or the train was crowded, and then he'd pull them into whichever car was closest or emptiest, and Jennifer and Ben would spend the ride scuffing their feet, staring at strangers' backs and poking each other in the ribs, all the while wishing they were up front, flying.

He wraps his arms around the pole, rolling his skateboard back and forth under one foot, and imagines the tunnels filling up with water. There'd be no way he could swim through them, but he pretends he could, pretends he is a better swimmer than he is, sees his arms moving in strong arcs, his legs kicking, forming a current that bubbles behind him. He swims beneath Manhattan, out into the East River, and keeps going, breaking free, leaving the ruined city behind.

When the train pulls into the next stop, he realizes he's been holding his breath. He exhales in a rush, growing light-headed.

After the diner Sandra kissed him on the cheek, her breath thick with coffee. "See you later, kid," she said and slipped inside her building, the door locking behind her. She'd given him no invitation, not even a chance to slip in behind. He stood on the stoop and considered buzzing her saying he'd forgotten something, but he didn't want to seem desperate. He'd be mature, give her some time, some space. A chance to get rid of Trey.

Anyway, Ben had things to do. Like buy a lock for his room. He decided to go home and get the money from beneath his mattress; the time had come to stop saving, start acting. Heading toward the subway, he felt a sense of purpose: he'd get Sandra in on his plans, show her how smart he was, how resourceful. She'd be impressed by what he could accomplish, what they could accomplish together.

But as he gets off the train at Seventy-Second Street and plods up the stairs, he becomes filled with dread, picturing the dark apartment, his mom in bed. He hopes that she's up and dressed, on her third cup of coffee, reading on the couch with one leg tucked under her and the other swinging, or rearranging the knickknacks on the bookshelves, or even sitting at the ugly desk in Jennifer's old room, going through the files he knows are there somewhere, lost beneath the mess.

Or, better yet, that his mom's not home.

The living room curtains, which Ben opened before he left in the morning, now stand closed. He drops his skateboard in the foyer. The thud echoes, but his mom doesn't shout in response. He peels off his sneakers, tosses them next to the skateboard. He'll be ready to go again in a few minutes.

Nothing in his room looks different, but the space feels opened, the air watchful. He closes the door and kneels next to his bed, slipping his hand beneath the mattress. The envelope is still there. Quickly, he counts—$275. Not nearly enough, but a beginning, at least.

On the way down the hall, he peeks into his parents' bedroom. The bed is empty, the sheets spilling onto the floor. Making the bed was the first chore his mom taught him. "A made bed means a day started right," she'd said, and he's always believed her.

He pulls the sheets up, tucks the edges beneath the mattress, props the pillows against the headboard, and fluffs them, the way his mom showed him.

He finds her lying on the kitchen floor.

"Mom," he says and nudges her leg with his foot.

A hand reaches up and claws the air. The hand finds Ben's arm, clutches it. She uses it to pull herself up, pull him down, until they are sitting side by side against the dishwasher.

"Hi, sweetie," she says.

"What are you doing on the floor?"

"How was"—she waves her hand toward the window, snaps her fingers—"Mike?"

"Fine." Ben touches the hem of her bathrobe, thinking about Sandra's green kimono. His mom's robe smells like the towels in the bathroom when they've been on the rack too long.

"I was about to text you," she says.

"Why?" He examines her more closely. Does she know about Sandra, her green kimono, what he'd like to do underneath it? The money in his pocket?

Blurry eyed, she smiles at him, and he understands that she knows nothing. Only what he tells her.

"I just missed you," she says.

"Have you eaten today?"

She stares blankly.

Ben goes to the refrigerator and takes out bread, turkey, mustard, ketchup, pickles. He stands at the counter above his mom and assembles a sandwich like the ones she used to make him after school. A dagwood, she called it, although he never understood why. He hands her the plate but can't lower himself back down to sit beside her on the floor.

The blinds are up. That, at least, is a good sign.

"Can I open the curtains?" he says.

"Which ones?"

"All of them."

She shakes her head.

"Just the living room."

She is tearing the sandwich apart, nibbling. A waste of food.

"It's better for the furniture to have them closed," she says.

"We didn't used to."

Putting the plate on the floor, she leans her head back, looks up at him.

"Come here," she says.

He doesn't want to, but he kneels next to her. She wraps her arm around his shoulders, pulling him close. His knees slide until he is sideways, almost in her lap. His arms go around her for balance, and he feels how she has changed, the bones where flesh used to be. She feels like a stranger.

She kisses his cheeks.

"Mom."

He shuts his eyes. Through her robe he can feel her beating heart against his neck.

"I have to go," he says, softly.

She cradles the back of his head with her hand.

"Mom." He jerks away.

Her hands fly up and freeze next to her face.

"I have to go."

Her mouth forms an O, and he is sorry for the harshness in his voice but doesn't know how to keep it out.

"I'm not sure when I'll be back."

She folds her hands in her lap. "Before seven," she says and nods, solidly, once.

The curfew is arbitrary. He knows that seven will come and go and she won't notice.

"Okay," he says. "Sure."

In the foyer he puts on his shoes and waits. Some memory of the past—of the person she used to be—tells him that she will rush out to remind him of something he's leaving behind. When she doesn't, he goes back into the kitchen. She hasn't moved.

"Get out today," he says. "Do something. All right?"

"Of course, sweetie." She smiles at him. "I was about to do just that."

Nine

"Leave me alone."

Carol says it louder. She shouts, her voice ringing off the walls of the empty kitchen.

"Just go away and leave me alone."

She bites her lip. She doesn't mean it.

For her son, she'll make an effort, get outside like she promised. Maybe she'll go shopping—you can't get more normal than that. She'll try on a floppy, bedazzled hat or a pair of outrageous plastic sandals in a neon color and take a picture. She'll text it to Ben. *What do u think? Should I buy?* Or, simply, *Y, N, M?* She will make her son laugh. He'll show the text to his friend Mike. "Your mom," Mike will say, shaking his head. That Mrs. Bauer. What a hoot.

In the bedroom she puts on yoga pants and Jennifer's yellow T-shirt. Her leg itches, and instead of scratching it bloody, she gets out the good lotion, Kiehl's, part of a gift set Drew gave her for Christmas, and slathers it on. She remembers deodorant.

In the elevator, when she looks down and sees that she isn't wearing shoes, she laughs so hard she pees herself a little and gets a stitch in her side.

Last night she painted her toenails while sitting on the bathroom floor. Sunburst Seduction: fire-engine red. *Slutty,* she thought, stretching out her legs, pointing her feet, but she took the word back. Not slutty. Sophisticated. Daring. Jennifer would love it. The makeup bag in Jennifer's apartment had contained crimson lipsticks, shimmery eye shadows, fake eyelashes, gold and silver glitter in little tubes. In a bathroom cupboard Carol had found hair extensions laid out like animal pelts. Sandra had taken everything. One day the artifacts of Jennifer's beauty had been there, and the next, they were gone. Carol noticed the glitter on Sandra's cheekbones and tried not to feel jealous. After all, Sandra is Jennifer's best friend, and she is young, entitled to beauty.

Last night Carol had been beautiful, too. The man had said so; she had passed a test.

Sunburst Seduction. If only Jennifer could see her mother now, barefoot, toes gleaming against the dull paisley carpet. They'd laugh together, clutching each other's arms.

The elevator doors open, and the two Greenberg children on the third floor enter with their nanny, a twentysomething Caribbean woman with enviable eyelashes.

"Hello," Carol says, and the children startle. The nanny smiles, eyes downcast, and pushes the button to close the doors.

Carol tries to remember the children's names. The boy leans against his nanny, but the little girl, a year or two older than the boy, steps forward, staring at Carol's feet.

"You're not going out like that," the girl says.

"Layla," the nanny says, "don't be rude."

"Oh, I don't mind." Carol lifts her foot, twirls her ankle. "Do you like the color?"

"You shouldn't go outside without shoes."

"Why not?"

"Because it's *not* what we do."

"Layla," the nanny warns.

Carol becomes aware of the sweat beneath her armpits, pooling around her breasts.

"No, it's okay," Carol says. "She's right. It's not what we do."

The little girl watches her with wide, wary eyes, as if at any moment Carol might strip off the rest of her clothes.

The doors part, and the nanny ushers the children into the lobby. Carol pushes the "Sixth Floor" and "Close" buttons simultaneously. As the elevator jolts up, she slumps against the wall.

Inside the apartment, she hesitates. From the foyer she can see down the hall to where her bedroom door stands open.

She is so tired. So heavy.

She could slip into her room, slip between the sheets, sleep, and the day would pass without her. The relief brings tears to her eyes—she doesn't have to keep going.

But she promised Ben.

On the credenza, there's her cell phone, her purse. All the things she needs, left behind.

"One," she says, a warning in her voice, the way she used to count down for Jennifer and Ben when they were running late for school and wouldn't put on their shoes, busy horsing around.

I'll give you until three, and then, trouble.

"Two."

If she were Ben, she'd be moving. If she were Jennifer, she'd be waiting, like this, testing the line, knowing the countdown would be started over.

Carol takes a deep breath.

"Three."

She grabs her phone, her purse. She hurtles to the closet, knocks her feet into a pair of flip-flops. She slams the apartment door behind her.

Ten

She is odd-looking, Drew remembers now, the repulsion he felt at their first meeting returning to him as Sandra peers around the door. He had expected Jennifer's best friend to be attractive, healthy, like her friends from high school, correctly proportioned with shiny hair and a bright complexion. Not this stunted, feral creature. He has to look down to see Sandra looking up, and she is nothing but dilated eyes: black unblinking rounds, little rings of green.

"Yes?" she says. "What can I do for you?"

Her tone is not unfriendly, but she keeps one hand on the doorjamb, the other on the door. She wears a threadbare kimono. Her skin is dull, as if she has not seen the sun in weeks. Of course, a diet of booze and pills would be deficient of every vitamin.

"May I come in?" Drew says.

Sandra glances behind her at the stairs. The door closes, just an inch, before she pulls it open, steps aside, murmuring, "Yeah, sure, please."

She leads the way upstairs. The walls are close, an ugly shade of tan that has a sheen to it. An array of stinks—cat litter, burnt toast, cigarettes—clogs the stairwell. At her door, she pauses.

"Give me a second," she says and disappears inside.

He folds his arms, wondering why he is being made to wait. He hopes she is changing; through her kimono, he could see the outline of her breasts, the erect nipples, a hoop through one. From the apartment he hears voices. One voice. Hers, low. He presses his ear to the door, but it starts to open and he jumps back, trying to refold his arms and missing so that when she beckons him inside, he is hugging himself.

The apartment is miniscule: a nook of a kitchen to the left, a bright-yellow curtain hanging at the back to separate out a bedroom. She sits down on a purple-cushioned papasan, and he takes the patchwork love seat. The cushions are too soft; he sinks down, so that when he looks across at her, she seems to float above him.

She twists one leg around the other, clasps her hands on top of her knee.

"Yes?" she says again, and he knows that she wishes he were anywhere but here.

Me, too, he thinks. *Me, too.*

The coffee table consists of a board supported by two concrete blocks, the surface crowded with candles, the cheap kind found at the dollar store, glass tubes decorated with the faces of saints, prayers for money, love, good health, general salvation. He remembers the candles from Jennifer's apartment, an incongruous collection that made him uneasy, reminding him of the candles his grandmother used to light at church. They were scattered across every room, even on the back of the toilet, half a dozen grouped on the windowsill next to Jennifer's mattress. Since then they have been corralled and have multiplied, at least doubling in number. Or maybe half were here already, the collection divided between the two apartments, like those cheap friendship necklaces Jennifer and her best friend of the moment used to wear.

In the candles' midst, he notices a lighter and a glass bong. The bong looks expensive. He had a roommate in college who owned one similar. Handblown. The smooth surface felt good cupped in the palm.

He yearns to hold Sandra's, to bring back that sensory memory. Instead he looks up at Sandra's collages. They make no sense, but he would never claim to be an art expert. To him, the collages are just bright blasts of color, the work of a child trying to shock. Pictures cut jagged from magazines. Legs and torsos, headless. Heads, bodiless. Sentences taken apart and rearranged until their intended meaning was lost.

He understood Jennifer's photographs better. Those, at least, shared commonalities with his life. He especially liked the shots she took in the subway. The trains a blur. People caught off guard, their faces open, unsuspecting, their emotions raw. Looking at the photographs felt voyeuristic, almost illicit. The vulnerability of the city exposed and put on display by his daughter. Jennifer conquering New York.

He was not happy when she dropped out of college after the first semester. For weeks he and Carol fought. Art was not a viable career path, he argued, not realistically. Jennifer would be dependent on them for the rest of her life. But now, looking at Sandra's collages, he thinks he might have been mistaken. Jennifer demonstrated real talent. Maybe she could have been one of the rare few.

Sandra taps her heel against her calf. Her hands open and shut on top of her knee.

Drew clears his throat, ready to begin.

Behind the curtain a floorboard creaks.

"Is someone else here?" Drew asks.

Sandra frowns.

"Trey," she says.

The curtain pushes back. A young man—Trey, apparently—emerges, looking like a punk in leather pants, a denim jacket, and combat boots. A crude tattoo of a dragon curls around his neck.

The company she keeps.

"This is Jen's dad," Sandra says and reaches toward the coffee table. Drew thinks she is going for the bong, but she picks up a stick of incense, lights it, waves it in a circle above her head. The room fills with a spicy scent, which triggers another memory of college, a girl Drew slept with on occasion who wore silver bangles along her arms and sang Joni Mitchell songs quietly to herself as she dressed in the morning. Her name was Maggie.

"Hey, man," Trey says, stooping, stretching his hand across the table. "Hey," he says as Drew stares at his hand.

"You're a friend of my daughter's?"

"Sure. She was awesome. Jen."

Drew notices the past tense. He is guilty of it himself, but he resents this kid even more for it. Trey puts his hand in his back pocket and looks at Sandra, who is holding the stick of incense beneath her nose. "I'm sorry, man," he says.

"Of course you are."

Sandra plops the stick of incense into an empty beer bottle on the floor beside the papasan and goes to Trey, standing on tiptoe to wrap her arm around his shoulders. He leans down, and together they whisper, their heads turned away from Drew.

Drew tries to imagine Jennifer in this place, with these people. He can't picture her long legs stretched across this ragtag love seat. He can't see her manicured hand cradling the bong. She used drugs; he knows this—he is not naïve. He smoked pot, too, when he was her age. But he won't picture it, or whatever else went on within these walls.

"She wasn't your little girl anymore," Carol said, blaming him. But was his wanting to keep Jennifer innocent so wrong? Should he be faulted for trying to keep his daughter safe?

Sandra and Trey break apart. They stand side by side in front of the yellow curtain, a grotesque *American Gothic*.

"Nice to meet you," Trey says and bows at the waist.

Sandra walks him to the door. When she returns, her face is tight, annoyed.

"Jen," Drew says, trying out the single syllable, but it's not the name he gave his daughter. "We never shorten it."

"No Jenny when she was little?"

"Never."

"Well," Sandra says, as if something has been proven.

He looks again at the candles. There must be three dozen. How did the girls choose which saint, which spell? Or did they just grab the candles from the dollar-store shelf at random, one incantation as good as another?

"I came to talk about my wife," Drew says.

Incense smoke twists like a serpent around Sandra's head.

"Your wife?"

"I know she visits you."

"Not on, like, a regular basis."

"What about last night?"

"Last night?" She shakes her head. "It's been a month. At least."

He notices the tattoo on her wrist, flashing as she moves her hand. "What is that?" he says.

"What?"

"On your wrist."

"Oh." Sandra holds her arm up. "Do you like it?"

"No," Drew says. "I do not."

Impulsively, he picks up the bong. The glass is as cool and smooth as he remembered.

"You want to smoke?" Sandra says.

"No." He drops the bong in his lap.

"Hey, be careful," she says. "My friend made that."

"I don't smoke," he says, setting the bong back on the table.

"Do you want tea? You seem tense."

"I don't drink tea."

"What do you do?" Sandra laughs. "Green tea is very calming."

She goes to the kitchen and puts a bright-blue kettle on the stove, keeping her back to him until the kettle whistles.

"Why are you asking about Carol?" she says, handing him a teacup. She sits back down in the papasan.

Drew holds his face close to the steam. The cup is delicate, like something Carol would buy at an antique store.

"She went out last night," he says. "She was gone for hours."

"She probably went for a walk."

"It was after midnight."

Sandra shrugs, pointing and flexing her toes.

"I'm sorry I can't help you," she says.

"Do you go out with her?"

"Out?" Her feet stop, flexed. "Out where?"

Feeling unsteady, Drew nudges aside a candle, puts the teacup down. "I don't know. Out."

"Not that I remember," Sandra says slowly. "No."

"That you remember?"

"We don't."

"What do you do together?"

"What do you *think* we do?" When he doesn't answer, she grins. "We don't do anything. We talk."

"About what?"

"All sorts of things."

"Who was that guy? Trey?"

Sandra tucks her legs beneath her. "He's no one," she says.

"You're just young and having fun?"

"Why not?"

"So was Jennifer."

"What's that supposed to mean?"

Drew raises his palm. "I'm only making—"

"Well, you can stop."

The buzzer blasts.

Across the sea of candles, they size each other up.

"I'm not done," Drew says.

"Look, like I said, I don't know where your wife—"

"Give me fifteen more minutes."

Seeing the refusal on her face, he leans forward, grabs her hand across the table. He is surprised by how small and smooth it feels, a little girl's hand, in his own.

"Please," he says, and there again are tears, real this time. He concentrates on blinking them back.

She wraps her fingers around his.

The buzzer blasts again.

"All right," she says, not letting go. "Fifteen minutes, but then I've got to get back to work."

Eleven

The sound of the buzzer reverberates in Ben's ears as he steps away from Sandra's door. He crosses the street and looks up at her third-floor window, the purple bedspread that serves as a curtain. The window is open, the bedspread moving slightly in the breeze. He wonders if Trey is still upstairs, but he hears nothing beneath the street's quiet, picks up no change in the air.

Maybe Sandra has forgotten about Jennifer's photographs, her promise to him. She is always on the verge of forgetting. That's why she needs Ben, to remind her.

A car passes with the radio turned up too loud, a bass assault coursing through the pavement, shaking Ben's legs. He covers his ears with his hands and realizes how idiotic he must look. He lowers them.

He has another mission for today: the lock for his room.

Ben cannot claim the Lower East Side as his home—not yet—but he is beginning to understand its rhythms, its rituals and inconsistencies. He is beginning to fall in love. The affection was forced at first, a way to stay connected to Jennifer. He searched for her among the low-roofed tenements, in the concrete parks, down the pockmarked alleys. And she wasn't there. No matter how hard he tried, he could not bring her back.

But that didn't mean he couldn't share her love for this place. He learned the layout of the streets, the poetic names so different from the numbered grid that had formed the backbone of his childhood uptown, and saw how moving here could be like moving to another country, even though it was only a few subway stops away.

Here you could start over. You could reinvent yourself.

Someday—there's no predicting when—these streets will be covered again with water, and the water will not recede like it has before. Down here, you feel the peril. You understand that you are living on borrowed ground, on borrowed time, and so you must live that much harder, making every second count.

Ben can feel himself becoming braver, sturdier. He is done living everyone else's life. He wants to live his own.

When the water comes, he wants to be here, not up on his hill. He wants to be with Sandra, watching from her third-floor window, holding hands in the dark.

Ben finds himself in front of the store with the dead animals. He never intends to come here, yet here his feet carry him again and again. In the window a dusty cow skull sits beside a shadow-boxed mouse skeleton spread out on black velvet. A stuffed raccoon glares with beady eyes. An owl watches sleepily from its perch in the corner. The shelves are cluttered with petrified wood, trilobites, big chunks of amber with insects frozen inside. A single green light bulb casts an eerie glow over the display, better seen on cloudy days, but the rest of the store lies in darkness. There is no sign, no list of hours. Although the door is always locked, Ben tries anyway, relieved when the door doesn't open, afraid that if he went inside, he would want to pick up the bones. He'd want to put them in his pocket, carry them home, where he would spread them out on his bed. He'd lie down next to them and just feel their presence. He can imagine the heat they would give off, the radiant memory of being alive.

Ben stuffs his hands in his pockets. The raccoon's eyes are more sad than angry. Like the eyes of zoo animals—trapped. He wonders how often the person who owns this shop cleans. Living mice probably crawl over the shelves at night, confused by their fallen comrades, victorious when they nibble on the raccoon's fur and dart through the cow's eye sockets.

Ben has considered asking Sandra about the shop, but he is uncertain of where that conversation would go once it started. He isn't ready to talk about death, not yet, not directly. Sandra was supposed to go with Jennifer that night, but she had the flu. She stayed home instead, worked on a collage, went to bed early, slept until morning. All of this information Sandra volunteered herself, and Ben listened, holding each word away, as if it might stain if pressed against him.

Inside the hardware store hammers hang precariously overhead. Shelves tower so high a ladder would be needed to bring down the light bulbs and screws. The smell of adhesive is suffocating, but nice, too, reminding Ben of elementary school art projects.

Behind the counter an old man peers down, eyes magnified by thick lenses. He has one of the largest noses Ben has ever seen and wears red suspenders, a white dress shirt with the sleeves rolled above his elbows and yellow sweat stains beneath his arms.

"Leave that thing by the door," the man says, nodding toward the skateboard. Ben is by the door; the farthest anyone can venture inside is a couple of feet. He puts the skateboard down.

"I need a lock," he says.

"What kind?"

"For a bedroom. Something secure."

The man disappears through an open door to the right.

"Who you trying to keep out?" he calls.

Ben doesn't think he's supposed to answer. He watches the street through the glass door; a crack at the bottom warps the view, as if he's looking through water. A woman pushes a double stroller. Two college kids roll past on bikes, talking loudly. He wonders if his mom is still in her bathrobe on the kitchen floor.

"This do?" the man says, holding aloft a package containing a shiny gold doorknob.

"Can I get some duct tape, too?" Ben says. Duct tape is one of those things you're supposed to have on hand, just in case.

The man takes a long pole with a grabber attached to the end and reaches across the counter, removing a roll of tape from the wall above Ben.

"You know how to install this thing?" the man asks, lifting his glasses to inspect the orange price sticker on the lock.

"Yeah," Ben says, although now he's uncertain. He assumed there would be instructions.

"You a lock expert, huh? Know how to pick 'em, too? That what the tape for? A little reconnaissance?"

"No," Ben says quickly. He takes the envelope from his pocket, removes two twenties, more than enough, and places them on the counter.

"Joke," the man says, but he doesn't smile.

Ben grabs the paper bag, folds it under his arm, and turns, almost tripping over his skateboard on the way out. Safely on the sidewalk, he pushes off, flying down the block.

He takes the bag between his hands, feeling the outline of the lock, the duct tape. When the big storm comes, they'll have to seal the windows, crisscross the panes of glass so the wind won't knock them in. They'll need bottled water, canned goods, a crank radio. Beyond the candles, Sandra isn't prepared, and those were bought for decoration, not protection.

Ben will show her. He'll set them up, and they'll be ready.

He stops at a bodega and buys six cans of beans, a gallon jug of water. He can barely carry it all. On the skateboard, he wobbles, his balance thrown off. His progress back to Sandra's is slow, but despite everything weighing him down, he feels light; he feels like the spring air.

Twelve

The tea makes Drew sleepy. He considers the possibility that Sandra has drugged him. As she curls up like a cat in the papasan, the kimono rides up, exposing her thighs, and there is something sexy about her, despite the piercings, the pallor. Something elusive and watchful, full of scorn. A woman certain men would fall over themselves to please.

Grabbing her hand had been unexpected; her fingers curling around his even more so. He is ashamed by how much her touch meant to him, the emotions it evoked. When he takes Carol's hand, her fingers lie limp, dead to his touch.

Desperately, he wants to explain himself. He wants Sandra to listen.

"I don't know what she told you—"

"You might be surprised," she says, picking at her fingernail. "You're not our main topic of conversation."

Already she has closed herself off. It isn't fair, the way the women in Drew's life move away from him, leaving him behind.

"Jennifer," Drew says. "Not Carol."

"Her either."

Drew rests his head on the back of the love seat. "We've had our problems," he says to the crack running along the ceiling, "but I'm not a bad father, and I'm not a bad husband."

When Sandra doesn't respond, he looks up. She has her legs stretched out, pointing and flexing her toes again, some sort of exercise.

"You're barking up the wrong tree," she says. "I honestly don't care if you're good or bad, whatever." She swings her feet to the floor. "Now, if you don't mind, I have work to do."

As she bends to pick up his teacup, he sees down the front of her kimono, the small swell of her breasts. The body of a teenage girl on a grown woman. He looks up, into her face. Her expression is unreadable; she does not meet his eyes.

"I don't know anything about her," he says.

"Your daughter or your wife?"

The question stings.

"Jennifer," he says. "Tell me something."

"Okay." She rocks back on her heels, the teacup held between her hands. "Here's something: Jen liked to go to this Cuban place for rice and beans at three in the morning. It was like a tradition. Even if we were just here, working, and awake at three, she'd want to go. We'd share a plate and watch the people. She made up names for the ones we saw over and over. Like this one, this transvestite who always wore a straight black wig and these gorgeous dresses. She was so elegant. We called her Cleopatra. Jen was jealous of her. I never saw her get jealous of anyone else."

"Why was she jealous?"

"Cleopatra was a queen," Sandra says, as if the answer were obvious.

Sandra carries the teacup to the sink. He tries to make her words form an image, but the cross-dressers he has seen have been over-the-top, crass parodies, nothing Jennifer would envy. The story doesn't make sense.

Drew takes out his notebook.

Who is this woman?

He looks across the room at Sandra's shoulders, as straight as coat hangers beneath that awful green kimono. On every wall her collages scream for attention, a kaleidoscope of the deranged.

All these colors—it's like being inside a clown's brain.

How could this have been what you left us for?

"What are you doing?" Sandra says.

He stuffs the notebook back into his jacket pocket.

"Are you a writer?" She takes a step closer, and he sees interest in her eyes. For a second, he's tempted to tell her what she wants to hear.

"No," he says, "it's nothing. A list of things I have to get done." He puts his hand over his chest pocket, where his phone remains silent. Where is the body now? How are they transporting it? He never thought to ask. Picturing a truck idling on the Jersey Turnpike, he shudders.

Sandra is watching from the kitchen alcove. He heaves himself out of the love seat, but he can't go yet, not without asking.

"Did Jennifer really hate me?"

Sandra plops back onto the papasan. "I was supposed to go with her that night," she says. "Did you know that?"

"Why didn't you?"

"I was sick. Do you hate me?" She taps her finger against the center of her chest. "Is it *my* fault?"

"If you'd been there, she wouldn't have left with him."

"Maybe. Maybe not."

"You wouldn't have let her."

"I did before."

Drew feels sick: the cloying incense, the too-close space.

"Then you weren't much of a friend," he says.

Sandra sets her jaw, and he feels brief satisfaction: a blow, delivered.

"Go home to your wife," she says, staring past him.

Drew leaves Sandra's apartment but doesn't go home. He goes to a bar with black walls and a low ceiling that makes him duck his head. He takes the stool at the end, next to the jukebox. As "Dream On" plays, he watches the jukebox lights turn from yellow to blue to green.

"Jack and Coke," he says to the bartender, who has the clean, open face of a baby. Drew used to like Jack and Coke, but he's been tamed by age and domesticity, limiting himself to white wine at dinner, a beer now and again at work lunches, avoiding the middle-age paunch. He can't remember the last time he got good and drunk.

The expected characters surround him: sagging old men; a woman in a tight gold top talking animatedly to the small, ponytailed man to her right; a young man in a business suit by the door, his tie loosened. Drew loosens his own tie in a show of camaraderie. The bartender sets the drink in front of him, and Drew takes his tie off. He considers throwing it on the sticky floor. Instead he lays it on the empty stool beside him, along with his jacket.

The Jack and Coke tastes sweeter than he remembered. He wonders how many he will have to down to feel it.

He used to see Jennifer everywhere. On the subway at rush hour, squeezed against a pole. Walking ahead of him on the street. On line at the deli where he buys his turkey sandwich every Wednesday for lunch. A few times, he even shouted her name. Once he ran and grabbed her shoulder, but of course the angry face that turned to him was not hers. He muttered an apology and slunk away, and later he thought about that woman's father, wondered how often the woman called him, how often she visited. He was jealous of the future they would have together: the wedding, the grandchildren. Happy family, sentimental stuff, images from commercials. If Jennifer were still around, she and Drew might have resolved their differences by now, but probably not. He is nothing if not a realist.

His glass is empty. He raises his finger for another.

As he waits for his drink, he swivels on his stool, taking in the scene, reveling in it. He can't imagine Carol in a place like this. She used to be a meticulous cleaner, even with Vera coming every Wednesday, although Carol put a stop to that months ago, saying she couldn't stand having a "stranger" around the apartment. The old Carol would vacuum the floors before going to bed, scour the bathrooms twice a week. Borderline obsessive, but he didn't care. He appreciated a well-ordered home. He liked knowing that if he dropped a piece of food on the floor, he would incur no harm in picking it up and eating it.

Now the dishes pile up. The laundry hamper smells. When he walks barefoot, crumbs stick to the soles of his feet. Two weeks ago he drew a frowning face in the dust on the living room bookcase. It's still there.

He hasn't mentioned any of this to Carol. She would become furious, tell him to do the cleaning himself, even though she's ignored his carefully worded suggestions to bring back Vera. But that isn't the point.

He holds the drink in his mouth, swishes it around.

What would his wife order? At home she sticks to sweet whites. Mild flavors. She sips slowly. She makes a ritual of pouring, nursing the glass. Deep in contemplation, running her slender fingers up and down the stem.

If she were to come in right now, he would watch from a distance. He'd observe the stool she chooses—would she stay to the edge or insert herself right in the center of things, elbowing a place between the old man in the cowboy hat and the one in the gray sweatshirt, giving each a friendly nod? Would she have to tell the bartender her order? Or would he already know, the drink half made by the time she crosses her legs and gives him a smile?

Despite himself, Drew becomes aroused. He shifts on his stool and stares hard at the wood grain of the bar, trying to expel his desire for this new, strange version of his wife, with her slim-fitting black dress, her loose hair, her red lips and darkly shadowed eyes. She moves her hands with limp wrists and snappy fingers and throws her head back, laughing at whatever joke the bartender whispers as he sets down her drink, his lips pressed wetly against her ear.

Drew waits for her to notice him. If after a while she does not, he will sidle up alongside her and wrap his arm around her waist. She will turn, her knees knocking into his groin, her red lips forming a circle. Her brow will furrow even as she smiles, because she thinks she is in trouble. Drew won't say a thing. He will take her hand, pull her off the stool, and lead her to the bathroom, where he will press her up against the cinder-block wall, between the toilet and the overflowing trash can, and yank up her dress, watching their reflection in the streaked mirror.

She is not there. The jukebox is playing "Knockin' on Heaven's Door," and he is at the bottom of his glass, again. He slides his tongue along his teeth, where the sticky sweetness has made a scrim, before gesturing for another, no Coke this time.

Thirteen

"Doctor's appointment," Carol said as she waved to Rob the doorman. His smile didn't balance out his squint of confusion, but she'd laid the groundwork, if Drew were to ask. Now, on the sidewalk, beneath the blinding sun, she almost goes back inside, but how to explain herself? She looks over her shoulder, and there is Rob in the vestibule, watching her. She can't shake her suspicion that Drew has asked him to spy. Rob's a good kid; his intention would never be to do harm. But Drew is the one who knows the baseball scores. He's the one who writes the holiday checks. Carol forces a grin in Rob's direction and makes a mental note to bake him chocolate chip cookies.

Needing to choose a direction, she looks east toward Broadway. She used to find the crowds exhilarating, threading her way around the slow movers as she sped through her errands. She'll go there now, to Fairway, and buy the week's groceries in the store instead of ordering online from FreshDirect. If she runs into a neighbor, a mother from school, so be it. She won't hide behind the shelves. She won't sneak around the aisle and out the door. She'll stand there with her head held high and say hello, and when they ask how she is, she'll say fine, without breaking down, without feeling resentful. *How are you? I'm fine. You?* Like any normal human being.

But her feet don't move.

She takes out her cell phone, checking for a text from Ben, a call from Drew, and remembers Julie's voice mail.

Julie: the bubbly former cheerleader, the sort of girl she would have hated in high school but a friend, a font of optimism since they met during the PTO kickoff meeting when both their youngest were in third grade. That's why Carol didn't return her message, or the half a dozen that came before it. Julie means well, but Carol couldn't suffer through the encouragement, or worse, that awful recitation: "You're going to get through this." But before, Carol liked Julie. They used to go to lunch every couple of months, sometimes shopping afterward, for the kids or some new piece of furniture Julie wanted Carol's design opinion on or just for fun. Julie had a way of drawing out whatever they were doing so that it filled the entire afternoon.

The message is weeks old by now, maybe even months. Carol checks her voice mail, but the only messages are from Dr. Rubin, inquiring about the missed appointments. It doesn't matter; she remembers the gist: Julie's husband inherited a pair of armchairs, and she wanted Carol's help incorporating them into the room. The prospect of a design challenge invigorates Carol—she hasn't used those muscles in far too long—and she spins around and heads into Riverside Park.

She almost jogs the eight blocks uptown, dodging dog walkers and strollers, a man in a ragged suit playing the trombone, a woman with her arms outstretched like a scarecrow, laden with shopping bags. The sun glints off Carol's nail polish, and she wishes she had spent more time on her hair, put on lipstick, so her toes wouldn't contrast so completely with the rest of her look. But if she turns back now, she'll lose her momentum. She will tell Julie that she is on her way to yoga class, or better yet, just from. Julie will understand. Carol helped design the yoga corner in her bedroom, matching the silk meditation pillows to the aquamarine mat, selecting a calming beach scene, all pastels and suggested cool breezes, for the wall.

The living room was Carol's crowning achievement: a leather sofa, Jacobean end tables in darkly stained oak, a matching library bookshelf, gold lamps. "Classic" was Julie's guiding principle, and she followed every one of Carol's suggestions, even when Carol nixed the coffee table Julie had picked out (that pedestrian glass top, a gathering place for fingerprints). Carol hopes for sedate chairs, something that will blend into the background and not displace the equilibrium. A light-colored upholstery. Simple lines.

The door to Julie's building stands open, the doorman helping an elderly man into a cab. Carol takes the opportunity to slip inside, around the corner, and up the stairs to the second floor. She stops at the top, seized by the sudden realization that Julie might not be home. She should have called first. She could still call. But what would she say? *Hi, I'm right outside your door?*

She tucks her hair behind her ears and knocks.

"Oh!" Julie says, opening the door wide. "I thought you were FedEx."

She is wearing yoga pants, too, and a tank top, her curly hair in a ponytail.

"I got your voice mail," Carol says.

"My voice mail?"

"The chairs." Carol's face grows hot. She holds up her cell phone as proof. "I was just down the street, so I thought—"

"Of course, dear." Julie grabs her, pulls her into a hug. "It's great to see you! Have you lost weight?"

"A little."

Carol waits for a compliment, but Julie just nods, lips pursed.

"Look," Carol says, pointing her toes, first the right foot, then the left.

"Fancy. Well, come on in." Julie leads the way into the living room. "Sorry I'm a mess. I wasn't expecting company."

The chairs are awful, two hulking mustard-colored travesties flanking the sofa. Carol kicks at the big bun feet.

"They were Henry's nana's," Julie says with a shrug.

The upholstery is as rough as sandpaper.

"They have to go," Carol says.

"Maybe a slipcover?"

"No. The structure is all wrong. See, it doesn't—what happened to the lamps?"

"The gold just seemed too much." Julie touches the base of one of the new lamps, slinky and silver, like an oversized insect.

"Too much how?"

"You know. A bit old school."

"The bookcase ladder—"

"Broke. It was kind of flimsy. Anyway, we decided we like it better without. A little less fussy." Julie pulls a chain, and a soft glow emanates from the insect-lamp's head. "See? Isn't that nice?"

Carol turns back to the chairs. "You can't tell me you like these."

"Henry would kill me," Julie says with a laugh, a flick of her wrist.

Carol looks down, at the Persian rug she helped pick out in a drafty warehouse in Queens. That, at least, is the same.

"What about the arrangement?" Julie says. "Maybe if we moved them."

"Moved them where?"

"I don't know. Over there."

Julie points vaguely toward the windows.

"I guess I've gotten used to them," she says. "Why don't we let it all gestate for a while?" She sits down on one of the offenders and crosses her legs, her left foot swinging. Carol sits on the sofa and runs her hand over the leather, still buttery smooth and cool against her palm.

"How about a drink?" Julie says.

She jumps up and returns carrying a silver tray with a wine bottle and two glasses on top.

"Riesling," she says. "Your favorite."

The gesture is sweet. Carol decides to interpret it as an apology. As she watches Julie pour, she tries to remember the names of her daughters. Once upon a time she and Julie spent hours together at card tables selling doughnuts and talent show tickets. They went to a diorama exhibit at the Museum of Arts and Design and ate salads in the café overlooking the park. They shopped for gifts at the Columbus Circle Holiday Market. What did they talk about?

"Cheers," Julie says and clinks her glass against Carol's. She rests her elbow on the arm of the chair and looks at Carol. She looks and looks.

"It really *is* nice to see you," she says.

"How are the girls?"

"Good. Becky's visiting my parents for break. Delia's still in Vermont."

Becky. And Delia.

"At school?" Carol says.

"Uh-huh."

"And she's liking it?"

"*Loves* it."

Carol sips the wine; it's perfectly cool, but the taste barely registers. "She's a freshman?"

"Sophomore. A politics major. Can you imagine?"

"But she loves it?"

"Well, you know, not all the time. There's stress. What everyone experiences."

"What *we* experienced," Carol says, and almost feels bad for the emphasis she puts on the word. "Boys," she offers as an explanation. Something they can commiserate on. Girls talking about boys.

Julie swirls her wine. "Well, there's one, but I don't think they're serious."

"What's wrong with him?"

"Oh, nothing's wrong. He seems a decent enough guy. They're just so young."

"You can't decide for them," Carol says, "can you?"

"How's Ben?"

"He's good. Enjoying break."

"And what about you?" Julie says. "What have you—"

"Been doing to pass the time?"

Carol notices Julie's chest move, her shoulders lift in a silent sigh.

"I keep busy," Carol says.

"Your business—"

"It's not quite there. Not up and running yet."

"I'm sorry I haven't been better at keeping in touch."

"You? I'm the one who can't return a voice mail."

"Dear, with everything you've been—"

"Oh, no, really, I'm fine."

Chin in hand, Julie nods, large brown eyes unblinking.

"I've been looking inward," Carol says. "And learning a lot. About me. And that's important. Right now."

She hates the way she sounds. Babbling. Pretending she's been going through some period of personal growth. She could be on *Oprah* or *Dr. Phil*. She could be reciting her therapist's maxims. After their first meeting, Dr. Rubin gave her a book: *A Mother's Grief Garden*. On the cover were purple irises against a pale-blue background. She was supposed to read the poems and journal on the blank pages. There were exercises that involved breathing. Carol read one Mary Oliver poem about geese and threw the book away.

I'm not grieving, she told Dr. Rubin. *I'm waiting.*

"Maybe I'll go off somewhere," she says now, her mouth still moving, unable to stop. "One of those meditation retreats. Not talk for a week or a month. Live on lentils. Let things go."

"My yoga teacher does that every year," Julie says. "There's a monastery upstate." She springs up again from the chair. "I know I have a pamphlet around here somewhere. Let me check my office."

Carol stares at the empty chair, the indentation Julie made in the seat. There was a time when Julie would have thrown those chairs out, whether Henry liked it or not, because Carol said so. She would have checked with Carol first before buying those ridiculous lamps.

74

Carol slips off her sandals. In this light the nail polish looks darker, a more benign shade, one Jennifer wouldn't bother wearing.

She listens for Julie, a shuffling of pages, a murmured conversation on the phone, the flush of the toilet, but all she hears is the ticking of the grandfather clock, also new, in the corner by the passageway to the kitchen. All these additions, like tumors, growing unchecked.

She leaves her flip-flops in front of the sofa and pads down the hall in bare feet, passing Julie's office, the door open, Julie standing at her desk. Carol continues on. She remembers the girls share a room across the hall from their parents. Here, at least, not much has changed, the walls still pale blue, the beds a matching set, twin white four-posters, one neatly made, the other not. On top of the dresser is a photograph of Becky and Delia at Delia's high school graduation. Delia wears a white dress, like Jennifer wore, and holds a single red rose. The sisters have their arms around each other, their heads pressed together. They look like Julie. They look like children should: unaware.

"Found it," Julie says.

Carol holds out her hand to receive the pamphlet. On the front a monk in a saffron robe sits in a forest clearing, long-haired women on either side, their eyes closed, their hands resting on their thighs.

"Wow," Carol says.

Julie leans against the dresser. "I know," she says, "flashback to 1969, right?"

The top of the dresser is littered with adolescent girlhood: hair ties, a bottle of perfume, a small stuffed penguin wearing a purple-and-white striped scarf, bracelets and necklaces in tangled heaps. Single earrings missing their other halves. Carol picks up a charm shaped like a ladybug. She rubs it between her fingers. Every spring when she was growing up, ladybugs would creep into the house. Her mother, terrified of spiders and ants, would never let her squash them. Ladybugs bring good luck.

"Do you want to talk about it?" Julie says.

Her eyes are wet.

Carol turns the pamphlet over, pretending to study the directions, the dates.

"If there's anything you need—"

"Just this," Carol says. "Thanks."

The silence extends, from awkwardness into discomfort.

"Well," Julie says.

Carol refuses to look up.

"More wine?"

As Carol follows Julie back down the hall, she realizes she still has the ladybug in her hand. She folds her fingers around it, pressing the metal into her palm. Settling back on the sofa, she opens her purse and drops the charm inside.

She checks her cell phone. There's one missed call, from Dr. Rubin's office. She swipes it away.

"Oh," she says. "Is it this late already?"

She sees relief pass over Julie's face.

"I'll call you," Julie says, reaching out as Carol rises, grabbing her elbow. "Think about the slipcovers. The lesser of two evils."

Around the corner, in Riverside Park, Carol lowers herself onto a bench. She takes out the ladybug charm, rotates it slowly between her thumb and forefinger. Across the path, boys shoot baskets, their ball making a gentle thump, thump. At the next bench over, a bald man in a teal tracksuit tosses birdseed. Pigeons flock at his feet.

In high school Carol wore a bracelet with six charms—a four-leaf clover, two hearts, a horse, a rainbow, a crescent moon—and she remembers the pleasing weight of the silver, the jangle whenever she moved her arm. The joy that sound would bring.

There have been dozens of missing girls, and at the end of the day, they have had nothing in common with Jennifer, except for their youth, their beauty, their lack of luck. Carol shuts the ladybug in her fist. It isn't fair, the way luck is distributed. The chances some people take for granted, the hopes others are robbed of.

She has done Google searches, following one link to the next, starting at mug shots of serial killers, reading their life stories. Reading the stories of women who escaped, who have gone on to live normal lives. Last night, at Inferno, she felt the closest she has to Jennifer since she disappeared. If she had just tried a little harder—stayed a little longer, not allowed herself to become distracted—her daughter could have been within reach.

Carol steps into the flock of birds. They fly up, spraying her with birdseed. The bald man curses, but she doesn't hear. She is thinking about the body she knows is not Jennifer's; she would give anything—give her whole self—to be right.

Fourteen

"What the hell am I supposed to do with all these beans?" Sandra says.

Ben stacks the cans on the counter beside the jug of water. "They're for emergencies."

"Right." Sandra picks up a can and begins peeling off the label. Ben stops her hand.

"We need to know what's what," he says.

"They're all beans."

"We'll get other stuff. Soup and things."

"Aye, aye, Captain."

Sandra still has on her kimono. Her lack of real clothes unnerves him, makes him think of his mom in her white bathrobe. He wonders what Sandra has been doing all this time. The curtain separating the bedroom from the rest of the apartment is pulled back, the bedsheets rumpled, the pillows askew, the quilt on the floor. He scans for traces of Trey, but the apartment looks the same as it always does. He fights the impulse to go over, make the bed.

"And what's this?" Sandra says, poking the roll of duct tape.

"For the windows. We'll need a radio, too. Do you have a flashlight?"

She stares at him, openmouthed. Ben puts the cans beside her canisters of tea in the cabinet.

"You really think we'll need this stuff?" she says.

"It's inevitable."

Since Jennifer disappeared, Ben has thought a lot about inevitability. Fate, some might call it. Jennifer could have stayed home that night. She could have gone over to Sandra's apartment with medicine and chicken soup. She could have visited her family. She could have called him and asked about his day, told him about hers, talked late into the night, making him tired for the errands his mom wanted to run with him in the morning. But she didn't.

Even if he somehow developed superpowers and was able to turn back time, who could say that Jennifer wouldn't make the same decisions?

No, human choice means very little in the overall scheme of things; the universe acts on its own accord. Someday the water will rise and submerge Manhattan. That is fate. But this is Sandra's home. She won't leave it, and neither will he.

Together, they will protect their small part of the world.

She slips the roll of duct tape around her wrist like a bracelet and gives it a twirl.

"What would I do without you?" she says.

They push the coffee table against the love seat, an effort that takes both of them together bearing the weight against their shoulders, and spread Jennifer's photographs across the floor. Ben has seen some of them before. Jennifer brought them to dinner in a binder, preserved behind cellophane. She slipped each one out and held it up. They were passed around the table: from Jennifer to Ben to their mom to their dad, who put them facedown, a stack next to his plate. Black and white. The steady silhouette of a pregnant woman in front of a blurred subway train. Two shirtless boys playing basketball in an alley, a flock of pigeons swooping close to their heads. A man in makeup and a wig, dressed in a sparkling evening gown, sitting on a park bench with ankles crossed beneath the glow of a safety light.

Their mom exclaimed over each one. "These are amazing, sweetie. Really amazing. This one—the expression on his face is so sad. I feel like I know him."

Their dad said nothing.

Jennifer glared. She stopped after half a dozen, slammed the binder shut.

"Well?" she said, and their dad lifted up his palms.

"They're pretty," he said, "but just think what you could have learned in college."

"They're not good enough?"

"I'm just saying you don't know. With proper training—"

And their mom grabbed their dad's hand, grabbed Jennifer's, so that she was stretched between them.

"Don't," she said, and to Ben's surprise, both of them stopped.

But most of the photographs Ben hasn't seen. There are dozens, most eight by ten, or nine by twelve. Two are large canvases, coming up to Ben's waist. One of these is of Sandra. She is wearing her kimono and sitting on a fire escape. It is night. The photograph is taken from above so that her face is not visible. A trail of smoke drifts from her cigarette out over the street, which is out of focus. Ben imagines Jennifer standing behind Sandra. She would have just ducked out of the window, camera in hand. Next to Sandra is a whiskey bottle, almost full, the cap off. There are leaves on the trees, a breeze catching Sandra's hair.

"We were at a friend's place," Sandra says, "getting ready to go out. I didn't know she'd taken the picture until she made it into this."

"Which friend?"

"I don't remember."

On the other canvas a man stands in a claw-foot tub, looking out a small window. Light streams in, haloing his body. Like Sandra, his back is to the camera. He is naked, his body firm, compact. He seems like he would be short. Across his back, a sunburst tattoo explodes.

Ben looks at the canvas and away. He looks again. The man does not fit Sandra's description of Trey. Ben can't stop thinking about his sister in the bathroom doorway, the camera pressed against her face. Did she sneak up? Did she ask the man to pose, direct his body where she wanted it to go? Had they just spent the night together? Or had they met up at an appointed hour just to take this picture?

He wants to ask Sandra but can't. She doesn't offer any details. She crawls around the floor, leaning down on her forearms to examine each photograph. Her legs tangle in her kimono. He stares at the dirty pads of her feet.

He keeps hoping he'll see himself. That Jennifer captured him in an unexpected moment. He wants to see what his body would look like, unsuspecting.

His sister was even more powerful than he realized—a shaman, collecting spirits. These photographs will be here forever, even though she's gone. He is thankful for them, for her foresight in taking them.

"You should choose," Sandra says. "I can't."

She sits against the far wall, next to the bedroom curtain, her legs stretched out in front of her.

Ben can't choose either. All the photographs should be shown, and none of them.

He goes to Sandra, sits next to her. They don't speak for a long time.

Sandra sighs. "Want to smoke?"

She packs the glass bong. The first time Ben pretended he knew what he was doing. As he hacked and hacked, she ran her hand over his back. Now that he can take the smoke into his lungs, hold it there with ease, he wonders how he'd ever not been able to do it.

"What we need to do," Sandra says, "is make two piles."

Ben leans his head against the wall. He can't pass judgment. He can't look at something his sister made and say yes or no.

"And we need to consider my collages," Sandra says. "The exhibit has to be cohesive."

She hands the bong to Ben and moves around the apartment, taking collages off her walls. He winces as she almost steps on the photographs.

When Ben closes his eyes, he sees the dead animals in the shop window. Solid and white, the mouse bones have grown to the size of a cat. The cow skull moves its jaw. The raccoon claps its hands.

In the flood, the animals will have nowhere to go. The glass window will burst against the pressure, and they will have to swim.

Ben cannot feel his own bones. They have left him. Inside he is vacant; he is nothing but air. He wonders if this is what the spirit feels like, untethered. If being high is akin to death, to life ever after.

Sandra spins around the room on her toes. Her movements make him dizzy; he wants her to stop. She is moving faster, getting inspired. The collages pile up on the love seat, and she is laughing, rising, falling, laughing. She is very much alive.

Fifteen

The woman in the gold top buys Drew a drink. At some point her little companion left and she ended up here, on the stool next to him. The young businessman is gone, and most of the old men, too, although some of them have been replaced by others.

Up close the woman appears even less attractive than she did from across the bar. Her front tooth is chipped, her lipstick on at a slant, her chin weak, hinting at past or future weight gain. But her body generates a comforting heat. She presses her arm against the length of his, their hands resting next to each other on the bar.

He doesn't catch her name, but she is telling him a story. She leans in close, her chin almost touching his shoulder, her voice confidential.

Drew sips his drink and decides to listen.

"It was alarming," the woman says. "I don't know how else to explain it."

Drew nods. What is alarming is the woman's hand on his knee, but the alarm is muffled, sedated. The hand is there for only a second. A pat, almost a smack. Drew looks up.

"Honey," she says. "You okay?"

"My wife," Drew says, and the woman's face bunches with concern. "I think she's with my daughter." But that isn't right, isn't what he meant to say. The sun has shifted; the angles on the bar have become languid, dripping off the edge. He stopped wearing a watch years ago, when he got a cell phone. Now he misses being able to glance down at his wrist. He sets his phone on the counter. More than two hours have passed—two hours with no messages left. He dials his voice mail, just to make sure, and listens to the electronic voice tell him that no one has needed him, nothing is an emergency.

The woman is drinking a beer. "Alarming," she says, addressing the bottle. "But I've never been one to complain."

Drew's laughter surprises them both. She narrows her eyes, but her lips twist into a smirk.

"What do you know about me?" she says, teasing.

"Nothing," Drew says. "I don't even know your name."

Now she laughs. "Honey, that's 'cause I never told you."

The old man two stools down braces his hands on the bar and rises slowly. Tossing down a bill, he shuffles away. The door opens, letting in the sounds of the street, stirring the close air. When the door closes, nothing has changed in the room except for one more stool being empty. Drew likes it here, the stasis. He tries to remember what the old man was wearing, but he can't bring a single detail to mind. The bill is pocketed, the empty glass whisked away, the bar given a quick rub with a white towel.

"You got a quarter?" the woman says.

Drew puts his hand in his pocket, and there, miraculously, is a quarter. She pinches it between her thumb and forefinger.

"Best deal in town," she says. "What else can a quarter get you in this godforsaken city?"

She spins around and pops the quarter into the jukebox. "Sweet Caroline." It isn't what he expected. She wobbles her head and sings along. Her voice is high, a little girl's voice.

When the song finishes, she lays out her palm and he places another quarter in the center. Her nails are long and black, with a silver star at the tip. Like the night sky.

Kenny Rogers sings about knowing when to walk away, when to run, and the woman sighs and says, "Ain't that the truth."

There's nothing left in Drew's glass. She notices, signals to the bartender.

And she is off again, hands flapping against the beer bottle. Drew watches her sloppy lips move. He watches the bartender leaning against the cash register, staring off into space with the white towel slung over his shoulder. He wonders if after being in such a dim space, the sunlight hurts the bartender's eyes. He imagines him walking through New York City with a perpetual squint.

"Hey." The woman pokes his shoulder. "You're not listening to a word I say."

She pokes him again, right in the stomach. He turns to her and opens his eyes wide, but his hand is searching for his suit jacket, finding the notebook, pulling it onto his lap.

"Black mold," she says. "Not just in the bathroom and kitchen but the bedroom, too. You know that was why I had that congestion. You know that's why I was tired all the damn time. And what do you think they did? Painted over. That's right. Nice white paint. Like it never happened. Like it wasn't still there growing underneath." She fans her hand across her chest. "I swear I can hear it. Multiplying. I sleep on the couch. What do you think of that? I can't even sleep in my own bedroom."

"Alarming," Drew says.

She shakes her finger at him, her night-sky nail coming close to his eyes.

"You," she says. "You." As if she has known him and recognized him all his life.

Just as suddenly as it started, her good mood stops. She plants her elbows on the bar and concentrates on drinking.

Drew takes out his pen. He taps the page, but something is stopping him. His memory has been blocked.

"What's that?" the woman says.

She leans over Drew's shoulder. Behind the smell of beer is another smell, defiantly, audaciously feminine.

Lilac. His mother would clip bunches every spring from the bush beside the front steps. He would take them to school, the stems wrapped in tinfoil, to give to his teachers.

He feels the pressure of the woman's knee against his thigh and realizes that he's sweating.

"Nothing," he says. "Just making a reminder."

"Go ahead then," she says.

They both look down at the blank page.

"I can't," he says.

"Write down my story. Someone ought to witness it." Using the bar as leverage, she rises partway out of her seat. "I call the city, but does anything get done? No. I'm left to sleep in contamination." She plops back onto her stool, looking about to cry. "I call and leave messages, and no one calls me back. And the times I talk to a real live person, they treat me like I'm no one. A number. Not even that."

She slams her beer bottle on the bar. It lands wrong, falls on its side, but that makes no difference—the bottle's empty. The bartender, sensing trouble, comes over to their side.

"Spin the bottle?" she says to the bartender, pointing. She gives the bottle a push, and it tumbles over the bar, out of sight.

"What am I going to do with you?" the bartender says, and the woman giggles. She actually giggles. Drew sits back and tries to take her in again. Maybe all this time she has not been flirting with him. Maybe she's just been another lonely soul searching for a time suck.

He is out of practice, no longer an expert, or even adept, at reading the signs. It used to be that Carol could say his name and make it sound special. She could look at him from across the room and speed up his pulse. When he touched the small of her back in a crowd, he sent her spine twitching. Once they had groped each other in his boss's daughter's bedroom during a holiday party. They had been craving and careless and ridiculously young.

The woman in the gold top is not Carol, not even close.

"My daughter," he says, and the woman and the bartender cease their conversation.

"What, honey?" the woman says, her knee returning to his thigh. "You mentioned her before. What's up with your daughter, honey?"

The bartender puts his hands on his hips and looks away.

"I think I'm losing them," Drew says. "I think I've lost her."

"Now, now. That's not so." The woman is saying the same thing to him as she'd say to any man, as she's said a thousand times before. "Nothing's lost until it's gained, honey."

He looks down at the blank page in his notebook. The woman and the bartender resume their conversation. Their words float above his head, tangled up in Three Dog Night's "Joy to the World."

Drew's phone rings, Morton's name on the screen.

Sixteen

Carol had to badger the police for the video; she never understood what harm it would cause, how it could hurt the investigation for her to be able to watch it as many times as she liked on her own. Detective Morton probably gave it to her to shut her up. Just as well. Carol has learned at this later stage in life how persistence can pay off.

In Jennifer's room, she keeps the lights off. She sits on the floor next to that inexcusable desk and opens her laptop.

At first, the clarity made her hopeful. The club invested in a good camera.

A slab of sidewalk. The bouncer beside a velvet rope, doing something with his phone, his feet planted far apart. No one on line. The night winding down.

Even though she knows what follows, Carol always holds her breath.

They come out together, Jennifer and the man, she on his left, her arm linked through his. Her long, light hair loose. She wears a short dress, her arms bare, in need of the jacket she left behind. Briefly, she rests her head on the man's shoulder.

He is taller by only an inch or two, athletically built. Short dark hair. A pin-striped suit. No face. He could be anyone. Carol could have passed him on the street. She could have sat next to him on the subway. He could be Dan, the man she met last night. Except that he is not.

Jennifer glances back once toward the camera. Her shoulder brushes against the bouncer, who does not look up from his phone.

The man with no face leads her around the corner.

She disappears.

Seven seconds, from start to finish.

Carol plays the video again.

Last night, Jennifer was there. Hidden within the black and red, inside the beat the DJ played, her lungs pulling oxygen in, releasing, so that Carol breathed her breath.

Her fingerprints on the tabletop. Her cells coating the glass, frozen inside the ice cubes.

Her heart beating, just out of earshot. Her voice, her laugh, just out of range.

Carol can find her, she knows she can, if she just looks harder.

Seventeen

In the cab uptown, Drew forces himself to visualize bones. Chicken bones, small and delicate. Dinosaur bones, large and indestructible. The skeleton that hung in the back of biology class in tenth grade, which Drew reconsiders now—it was too short, the size of a child.

His stomach gurgles, his drunkenness a disgrace. He should be sober for this, the most important task of his life. There were tricks he used to know: coffee; exercise; a big, greasy breakfast; making yourself throw up. All he can manage now are deep breaths, his forehead pressed against the cab window, his nausea increasing with each bump in the road.

He should call Carol. He goes so far as to take his phone out of his shirt pocket and put it in his lap, but he can't bring himself to do more.

The medical examiner's office is brightly lit, the windows letting in the late afternoon sun. Drew wishes for darkness, for corners to disappear into, for this day to be over, for it never to have begun. Morton is there, waiting for him in the lobby, with her sensible short haircut, her sensible pantsuit, her sensible round-toed shoes. She puts a hand on his elbow, the first time she has touched him or even come close.

"Drew," she says, and that is enough for Drew to break down.

They sit him in a room. There is a table, and a cup of coffee he can't remember asking for. Morton sits across from him, and beside her, a middle-aged woman with the comfortable bulk, neat honey-colored pageboy, and soft eyes of a preschool teacher. They have been asking him questions, but all he can think about is the manila folder beneath Morton's folded hands, the photographs inside.

"You don't have to view the body," Morton said when she sat down, as if that would bring him relief.

"I want to."

Morton's thumbs rubbed together.

"Can I?" Drew asked.

But there are rules. Policies. Drew respects order. He understands the need for procedure. Eventually the body will come to him. When the autopsy has been completed. When every last option has been exhausted. The body will come to him, and he will bury it. What is left.

If the body is Jennifer's.

"We know this is very difficult," the preschool teacher says. Drew has forgotten her name, why she is here. She slides a pamphlet toward him. A hotline number for grief counseling.

"I'd like to get on with it," Drew says, leaving the pamphlet where it is in the middle of the table.

The preschool teacher glances at Morton, who opens the folder. She places two photographs in front of Drew.

"She was well preserved," Morton says, quietly and with a sort of reverence, as if Drew should take it as a compliment, and for a brief second, reminiscent of his old life, when he could take pride in Jennifer's accomplishments—honor roll; first place in art contests at school; her scholarship to college; the crayon drawings she used to explain to him, curled up in his lap—he does.

The first photograph is of her face. The skin has sunk, her skull becoming more pronounced, but she is not reduced to bones, not yet. Her hair is matted. There are no bruises that he can see. No signs of distress. It is as if she fell asleep in the woods for a long time, as if she were put under some sort of spell.

"That's her," he says, because he has no choice. "That's my daughter."

By saying it, he claims her, he brings her back to him. He pulls the photograph closer. "That's Jennifer," he says.

The second photograph is a close-up of the tattoo. He pushes it aside.

"How?" he says.

"Strangulation, we think." Morton puts the photograph of the tattoo back in the folder. "An autopsy will be more conclusive."

Only a portion of her neck, unmarred, is visible. She would not have taken a picture like this. The lighting is wrong, too harsh. Or maybe she would have found beauty in that brutality. She could see beauty in places he could not.

"Who found her?"

"Hikers," Morton says.

"Hikers?"

"A man and a woman."

He wants more: their names, their faces, their life stories. He wants to be grateful, but instead the intimacy of his connection with these strangers unnerves him. They found Jennifer, by accident, something he couldn't do in a year of trying, hoping, giving up.

"Where?" he says.

"Central PA."

But Pennsylvania is so big; he needs more specifics. He needs to see the place.

"The back of a cave," Morton says. "Near Harrisburg."

Drew envisions a quiet forest path, the mouth of the cave easy to overlook among rocks and trees. Birdcalls. The soft pad of animal feet. The shifting of the seasons. He looks at the photograph, Jennifer's expressionless face. The thought of her body lying there for who knows how long fills him with unbearable loneliness. How could he have not known where she was? How could he have been going about his days as usual when she was waiting to be rescued? How could he have failed her so completely?

"We used to take day trips upstate," he says, "when she and her brother were little. They loved hiking. But we only went camping once. Her mother didn't care for it. Didn't like the bugs. Sleeping on the ground. We had these inflatable mattresses." He gestures, simulating the outline of a mattress with his hands. "But they weren't very thick."

Nodding, her lips parted, the preschool teacher leans forward. Drew doesn't want her in the room. He feels embarrassed for having cried, for saying irrelevant things.

"What do you need from me?" he says.

Morton takes out forms. Of course there are things to sign, declarations he needs to make. He grips the pen so hard he thinks he might break it, but the routine comforts him—the order in all of this madness. A way to move through it, to try to get to the other side.

When the preschool teacher reaches—nervously, it seems to Drew—for the photograph, he puts his hand on her wrist to stop her. It's an automatic reaction, and he immediately knows it is the wrong thing to do. He lets go.

"Thank you," he says to the preschool teacher. "Thank you," he says to Morton. He takes his suit jacket off the back of the chair, puts it on. "Thank you," he says again, to both of them, to neither.

"The restroom," he says, and the preschool teacher tells him down the hall, to the right. Morton scoots her chair back from the table, carrying the folder under her arm. She follows Drew out the door.

"We'll keep you posted," she says, and Drew nods, walking away before she can say more.

In the bathroom, he kneels, dry heaving, in front of the toilet. When nothing comes, he sticks his finger down his throat. He slumps on the floor and stares at the toilet paper dispenser, the green stall door, the paint chipped away, revealing the metal underneath. There is vomit on his suit jacket sleeve. He closes his eyes and listens to the pounding of his heart in his ears.

It's a long time before he can get off the floor. He washes his hands, the water turned as hot as it can go, and scrubs at his sleeve with a damp paper towel, leaving behind bits of white. His reflection in the mirror is red-eyed, red-faced. That won't do. He has to pull himself together, for Carol, for Ben.

He sucks in his breath, holds it. Counts to ten and lets go. He wipes off his face. He buttons his jacket with shaking hands, clenches his fists, releases, again and again, but the tremor won't go away.

Eighteen

Ben opens his eyes to see Sandra's dark hair fanned out across his stomach. She is lying on the floor, their bodies perpendicular, her knees drawn to her chest, hands balled into fists, eyes closed.

Gently, he combs his fingers through her hair. His fingers catch, and he freezes before deciding to go ahead and tug. She does not stir. He wraps her hair around his hand. It is so soft. He wants to bring it to his face, inhale, but he is afraid that if he sits up, he will wake her.

Dust motes swirl in front of the window. When he turns his head, he sees Jennifer's photographs, a sea of black and white. All of Sandra's collages are down, piled on the love seat, and the bare walls look strange, as if someone has come in and robbed them.

Sandra's eyes open.

"How'd you get to be so beautiful?" she says, but her lips barely move, her voice so quiet that Ben decides he has imagined it.

He can't stand to look at her. He concentrates on the shadows lengthening across the ceiling. She moves her head, and he feels the pull of her hair against his hand. He lets his fingers go limp; the strands unwind. His hand rests on top of her head. She is using him as her pillow.

They lie in a rectangle of sunlight; he feels as if he is submerged in a warm bath. *This,* he thinks, *is why cats spend their days moving from one spot of sun to another.*

"We're cats," he says, and Sandra grunts.

"Meow, meow," she says.

She stretches out, offering her stomach to the window. He scratches her scalp. She purrs.

"I don't want to go home tonight," he says because he can't stop himself from saying it.

"Then don't."

For her, it's that simple: do what you want to do; don't do what you don't.

He has loved Sandra since before he met her. She is the closest he can come to his sister, the two of them her survivors in a way his parents can't be. After Jennifer left home Ben missed her fiercely, her phone calls never enough. At school, or during the long evening hours when his dad watched Bloomberg TV in the bedroom and his mom read decorating magazines on the couch, Ben would wonder where Jennifer was, what amazing thing she was doing right at that moment. Sandra was there with her, and she has welcomed Ben in; she has claimed him as her own.

Sandra and Ben both know Jennifer is dead.

He felt the hollow as soon as his mom told him Jennifer was missing and realized that he had felt it for a while, a day at least, a concavity at the back of his consciousness, distorting everything, making him a little seasick. He hasn't told his mom or dad. Their lack of awareness angers him. How can they not feel the hollow? Did they love her so much less?

Sandra feels it. He knew she would. Last fall, searching for gum, he found her address on a scrap of paper in his mom's purse and showed up after school. When she opened the door, they both started crying.

Looking at her was like looking at Jennifer, and Sandra said the same thing to him. They reflected Jennifer back to each other.

That day, for the first time, he felt like he could mourn. He couldn't stop shaking. She wrapped him in her quilt and made him cup after cup of green tea, which he drank even though the tea tasted like dirt. They didn't talk much; just being in each other's presence was enough. The talking would come later.

"Come over anytime," she said, and so he has, after school, on the weekends. His parents don't know. They assume he's staying late to work on a science project or grabbing pizza with friends or skateboarding in the park. They think he's still the same kid he was before. It's better that way.

Sandra rises so quickly, it takes him a moment to register her absence, but she is no longer lying on his stomach. She is in the bedroom, kneeling on the bed, taking down the collage, the only one that he has never liked. Standing above him, she holds it up, triumphant. Against a black background, cutout women spiral, ending in a large red question mark. The women are missing parts. Some lack heads, others limbs; a few are only torsos. Ben looks behind Sandra, at the dust motes drifting. He wants to stretch out, be a cat again.

Crouching, she sets the collage on the floor.

"What do you think?" she says.

He isn't sure what she's asking.

"This is the one."

She props the collage up against the coffee table and goes back to sorting through the photographs. Ben notices a pattern. She is moving the photos with only one subject close to the collage, putting the others into a neat pile. She looks at him and grins, her tongue poking out between her teeth.

"Do you see what I'm doing?" she asks.

He nods. They are missing people, except they aren't. They are here, frozen inside the frame. Only Jennifer is gone.

"We shouldn't separate them," he says.

"We can't show them all."

"Why not?"

Sandra sits back on her heels.

"There are too many," she says.

Ben crawls over and kisses her.

Their hands stay in their laps, but she tilts her head, opens her lips. Her tongue is pierced, something he didn't know, the stud another secret for the two of them to share.

She stands up. His lips are still parted. He closes them. She wipes her mouth with the back of her hand and turns, stepping over the photographs, and gets two beers out of the refrigerator. She opens the bottles against the counter, hands one to Ben.

"We'll ask Trey," she says.

Her fingers drum against her side.

Ben sips the beer, the first he's ever had. The taste seems wrong, like the beer has gone off, but he keeps drinking, deciding that he'll grow to enjoy it, like the coffee.

"Why do we need to ask Trey?" he says.

"He *does* own the gallery."

She's never used this irritated tone with him before.

"His *parents* own the gallery," Ben says.

She sits on the love seat next to the pile of collages.

"Come here," she says.

She puts her arm around him, bringing his head down to her shoulder. Now her fingers comb through his hair. There is something sad about her movements, something making Ben sad.

"Duct tape and beans," she says.

"It's only a start."

"Right. A radio . . ."

"It's not stupid."

"No. You take care of me, and I take care of you. That's our deal, right?"

Ben hesitates, feeling tricked. "Yeah," he says.

"We shouldn't mess it up."

He doesn't want to mess it up. He can still taste her on his lips, her saliva mixed with his.

"Do you understand?" she says, and he nods, his chin knocking into the crevice of her collarbone.

"Good boy," she says, but the way she says it is sweet.

Nineteen

Carol is lying in bed, in her underwear, when the phone on the nightstand rings. She doesn't answer at first. Drew thinks she is out; he would call her cell. She closes her eyes and the ringing stops, only to begin again a few minutes later. She wants to be left alone; she wants to sleep, but whoever it is won't let her.

She rolls over, reaches for the phone.

"Honey," Drew says.

She finds her cell phone in the tangled sheets next to her—the volume is off. When did she do that? She tosses her cell onto the floor.

"I'm on my way home," he says.

"Did you go?"

A long pause.

"Yes."

"Is it her?"

"I'll be home—"

"Is it her?"

But she already knows—the exhaustion in his voice, the sadness he is trying to conceal. She catches sight of herself in the mirror above the dresser and feels helpless in her underwear, exposed to the world, unarmed.

"Yes," Drew is saying. "It's her."

He is there, breathing on the other end. Waiting.

"How?" She clamps a hand over her mouth.

Drew coughs.

"Strangulation," he says. "They think."

"They *think*?"

"An autopsy—"

"No," Carol says. "No autopsy."

"They have to—"

"No, no, no." Her head is shaking, side to side to side, hurting her neck. "No."

"Shhh," Drew is saying. "Shhh."

"Don't do that. Don't tell me to shut up."

"I'm not. I'm just—they need to find out what happened. They need to do everything they can."

"That they *can*?"

It is not enough.

Drew is quiet. She listens to his breath. The two of them, breathing without space for words.

Twenty

Before Drew can go home, he needs to sober up. He takes a cab back to Battery Park. The sun glints off the water, blinding him as he runs, suit jacket flapping, wing tips resounding flatly off the pavement. Pigeons scatter. A woman feeding her toddler animal crackers startles as he pounds past their bench. A man seated on the pavement selling bottled water pulls in his legs. Behind Drew the city expands. Workers pour out of their offices, the evening too pretty to stay late. The Staten Island Ferry lets out its low whistle, and people sprint, their dress shoes chafing, hoping to make it through the sliding glass doors in time. Even in their hurry, there is joy—that spike of adrenaline, a memory of childhood surging. Some had forgotten what their legs and arms could do. As the glass doors slide shut, the faster ones slip through, exchanging grins of relief, a shout of triumph. The others stumble to a halt. Breathing hard, they curse the security guards, who watch with impassive faces, already counting down the hours until they, too, are free.

Drew is aware of none of this. He has stopped thinking, stopped observing. He is only skin and blood, muscle and bone, working perfectly in sync. A human machine.

He will run and run until he stops—he may never stop.

He is alive, but his daughter is dead.

Twenty-One

Lying in bed, the covers pulled tight, a shroud, Carol admonishes herself: she should have known. Mother's intuition, and on some level, she did know, even if she would not admit it to herself.

She loved Jennifer too hard, too much, not to lose her.

She has read the news articles, the citations of scientific proof: microchimerism. The cells exchanged in utero create an indivisible bond; the selves are mingled, mixed. The sound of two hearts beating resonates in your ears, soothing you in the darkness. The danger is when you forget to listen, and one night, just over a year ago, Carol awoke gripped by the fearful knowledge that her daughter's hearing was going.

In the kitchen, she pressed her body against the window, curling around the phone as it rang. She waited for voice mail to pick up. When at last Jennifer said hello, Carol had to hold the phone away, suck in air, so that she could find her voice.

"Mom," Jennifer said. "What's wrong?"

Carol spread her palm across her chest, where the fluttering stilled.

"Sweetie," she said.

Outside a light rain fell, and she knew that it was cold. People slept on the sidewalk, shivering. Their city was not hers; it was not Jennifer's, but it was close. Too close. All that separated them were a few feet of brick, and what was that? Sand and clay. The ocean's waste materials.

"Are you at home?"

"I was about to go to sleep," Jennifer said. "Why are you awake?"

Carol shut the blinds; the kitchen lost its definition. She could be anywhere. She could be standing in the kitchen of her parents' house in Wooster, Ohio. She could be a child, younger than Jennifer, afraid of nightmares, sneaking around the house after her parents had closed their door, moving from room to room so that sleep could not find her. "I was thinking about Grandma," she said.

"What about her?"

She pictured Jennifer sitting cross-legged on her bed, the duvet the same one Jennifer had taken to college. They'd bought it at Bed Bath & Beyond, a blue-and-purple tie-dyed swirl that reminded Carol of the skirts she'd worn when she was Jennifer's age.

"What?" Carol said.

"Grandma. What were you thinking?"

"Oh." Carol ran the blind pull between her fingers. "She used to hate it when I got out of bed at night. She didn't understand insomnia. She'd tell me to count sheep. Sometimes she'd get fed up and lock the door to my room."

"She locked you in? Because you got out of bed?"

"Well. You remember what she was like. Old-fashioned."

"What if there'd been a fire?"

Carol had never considered a fire. She tugged on the pull, bringing the city back into the room. Raindrops shimmered on the glass.

"She would have gotten me out," Carol said.

"There might not have been time."

"She would have. A mother runs into the burning building."

"Not all mothers."

"I would."

"I know."

Carol had not seen Jennifer in over a month. She had stopped coming to Sunday dinner. It had been part of the deal—Jennifer could quit college, move downtown, pursue her art, anything she wanted, with Carol and Drew to support her, if she would still come home for a couple hours once a week.

"We miss you," Carol said.

"I've been busy. I can't always get away. Not every week."

"You could call." Carol thought about the first week Jennifer hadn't shown up, hadn't called or answered the voice mail and text messages Carol had left. Carol wouldn't let Drew and Ben eat. The eggplant parmesan had grown cold. "Forget this," Drew had said close to nine, taking a silent Ben with him to get pizza. Carol had sat at the table and waited ten more minutes before throwing the eggplant parmesan, the garlic bread, the chocolate cupcakes that were tucked in the back of the refrigerator, a surprise, into the trash. The next week, at seven o'clock on the dot, Drew had sat down at the table and heaped chicken and mashed potatoes onto his plate. He had looked grotesque, a glutton, lips glistening, hands churning.

"Dad and Ben will eat the leftovers," Jennifer said.

"Sweetie, it's not about the food."

Jennifer sighed into the phone.

Carol's parents had not tried to stop her from moving to New York. Her father had bought her a new suitcase, brown leather. Her mother had bought her full slips, half slips, packets of hose in nude, black, and cream. They had driven her to the airport and pecked her on the cheek with dry lips. Her father had slipped an extra twenty into her coat pocket. And that had been that.

Overidentifying, Drew said, an artificial word, crafted out of jealousy. It meant nothing.

"Is it because of your father? I'll talk to him."

"It's not Dad."

"Then what? Is it me?"

"No. Mom, I'll try to come by tomorrow. In the afternoon, okay?"

"I'll be here."

"I'm going to bed," Jennifer said.

"All right. Good night, sweetie. See you tomorrow."

"Honey?"

Carol dropped her phone. The cover popped off, skidded beneath the table.

Drew moved away from the door. He put his hand on her elbow as he stooped to pick up the phone. He snapped it back together.

"Thank you," Carol said and tried to stuff her phone into her pocket, but she was wearing a nightgown.

"Are you all right?" Drew asked.

Carol shrugged. She didn't like the weight of his hand on her arm, but she tried to accept it. That weight used to mean the world to her.

"Yes," she said. "I'm all right."

"Come to bed."

She let him take her hand. As he led her through the apartment, she closed her eyes, to see how he would guide her, if he would allow her to bump into the furniture, the walls. He returned her to their bedside unscathed, and when she looked up at him, he was smiling.

"Don't worry about Jennifer," he said, lying down beside her.

His lips, dry against hers.

No, she thought, *I won't worry.*

They made love quietly, quickly. She slid into sleep with his hand in her hair.

The next afternoon, a little after three, Carol was reading in the living room when she heard the elevator ding in the hallway. She put her book down. The footsteps were unmistakably Jennifer's: the sharp syncopation of high heels.

Jennifer's wet hair hung in long, heavy strips on either side of her face. She wore a man's pin-striped blazer and, underneath, a sky-blue dress that fell just below her knees. The material looked light, billowy, inadequate for the weather, the wind still holding winter's chill. She set her messenger bag on the floor and after a moment bent to unzip her boots.

Jennifer seemed smaller, her skin paler. She came toward Carol in bare feet, rubbing arms covered in goose bumps.

"Are those pillows new?" she asked.

Carol placed a pillow on her lap and ran her hand over the silk surface. She had liked the rust color, thought it went well with the cream upholstery, but now she had doubts. "Do you like them?"

"Yeah." Jennifer's eyes moved away from the pillow, to the coffee table, the bookshelves, as if checking for other alterations. Carol felt guilty again about Jennifer's bedroom, but Drew had been so certain. He had made her excited about the prospect of a new life, when she would be a real designer, an alternative to the gaping, shapeless future. And Jennifer never spent the night here anymore.

Still. They should have asked first.

"Please sit," Carol said and regretted the *please*, which emphasized her daughter's role as a guest. Jennifer didn't seem to notice. She didn't sit either. She stayed in the middle of the room, rubbing her elbows, staring at the bookshelves.

"Are you hungry?" Carol asked, and Jennifer shook her head. She turned toward Carol and blinked, as if surprised to see her mother there.

She sat down at the other end of the couch, drew her knees to her chest. She threaded her fingers through her toes.

"That's a pretty dress," Carol said.

"It's a friend's."

"The color suits you." *But it's the wrong season,* Carol almost added. *I can get you a sweater.*

"So," she said instead. "Tell me your tales of adventure." She smiled and pushed Jennifer's hair behind her ears.

"I've been working," Jennifer said, glancing at her sidelong.

"The coffee shop's giving you more hours?"

"I'm not there anymore."

"What happened?"

Jennifer shrugged.

"Did you quit? Were you fired?"

"Does it matter?"

"That wasn't a bad job."

Jennifer's feet fell to the floor. "See? This is why I don't come over."

"Do you need money? Is that why you came?"

"I can go—"

"No," Carol said.

Jennifer's arms were so thin. Carol resisted the urge to circle her fingers around them to show Jennifer what she might not be able to see.

"I wouldn't be doing my job as a mom if I didn't worry."

Jennifer ducked her head, hiding behind a curtain of hair. Carol hated when she closed herself off. Quiet, happy Ben never made Carol work like this. But he was the second-born, the boy, and Carol's love for him was not as complicated, not so vast. She knew it was wrong to play favorites, but she couldn't alter the intensity of her attachments. She was her daughter's mother.

She noticed something, a mark, on Jennifer's wrist.

"What is that?"

Jennifer held up her hand. A Celtic knot in black ink, the skin around it red, raw.

"Do you like it?" Jennifer said, an edge to the question. Carol was meant to say no. She wouldn't.

"What does it mean?"

"Love. My friend got the same one."

"A boyfriend?"

"No. The kind of love that lasts."

"The friend who loaned you the dress?"

"It's not a loan," Jennifer said.

Carol watched her daughter's profile. The friend's dress, the too-thin arms, the sallow skin and throbbing tattoo and messy hair—the details added up to trouble.

"Let me brush your hair," Carol said.

"What?"

"It's tangled in the back."

Jennifer stood. She walked toward the door, and for a horrible moment Carol thought she would leave. But she bent to open her bag, took out a brush. She sat on the floor between Carol's feet, just like when she was a little girl.

Carol began at the crown of her daughter's head. She made the strokes slow, even. The strands were drying, the dark blond turning fair. Jennifer's hair had stayed the same color since it had come in. Hairdressers marveled that it had never been dyed. They raved about her natural highlights.

Carol could feel Jennifer relax beneath the pressure of the brush. She could still do this—bring order. Make things right.

Jennifer sighed. She leaned back, her shoulders pressing into Carol's calves.

Carol brushed long after Jennifer's hair had untangled and dried. She brushed until Jennifer's hair shone. Until her wrist began to ache.

"All done," she said.

Jennifer looked up. "Now I'll do yours."

Carol patted her own hair, a bob, the way she'd worn it for the past decade. "Really?"

"Come on. Trade places."

They did. Carol submitted to the tug of the brush, wishing her hair were longer so the strokes could be languid instead of short, choppy. It didn't matter. Hair could grow.

"How's the photography?" she asked.

The brushing paused. "Okay," Jennifer said.

"When are you going to have that show?"

Jennifer dropped the brush into Carol's lap, stinging her thigh. "God, Mom. It's not that easy."

"What? What did I say?" Carol scooted around to face the couch.

"Have a show." Jennifer snapped her fingers. "Just like that."

"I'm sorry, but I thought that's what you wanted. I don't know how it works."

"It's a sensitive subject, okay?"

"Okay. We don't have to talk about it." Carol turned the brush over in her hands. There was her dark hair, mixed with Jennifer's light. She pulled it out, made a hard ball between her fingers.

"Sorry," Jennifer said quietly. "I didn't mean to snap at you. It's been a tough few weeks."

Carol nodded. She would not ask how. She needed to be patient, to let Jennifer open up at her own speed. Even after twenty years, knowing Jennifer better than anyone else, she had to remind herself of that.

"Let me make us a snack," she said.

"I have to get going."

"You just got here."

"I have an appointment."

"The doctor?"

"No." Jennifer toyed with the hem of her dress, bunching it, letting it go. The fabric wrinkled.

"For the road then," Carol said.

In the kitchen, she took out bread, cheese, two apples, a packet of trail mix purchased for Ben's school lunch. He liked the kind with M&M's. She looked at everything spread out on the counter, unsure where to start, what would satisfy Jennifer, what would fill her up. Carol had nothing to put it all in; a plastic Duane Reade bag seemed tacky. She had to convince Jennifer to stay and be fed here.

"Wine?" Carol said when she heard Jennifer's footsteps. "We have mostly white, of course, but I think there's a red in there, too." She laughed. "A hostess gift."

She liked the idea of sitting down with her daughter as two adults, sharing a bottle of wine. She should have had a bottle open when Jennifer arrived.

"When was the last time you had a party?" Jennifer said.

"Lord knows." Carol began slicing cheese. "I got this at the Greenmarket."

"I don't eat dairy anymore."

"Why not?"

Jennifer had her boots on. "I've just gone off it."

"Oh." Carol put down the knife. There was no denying it—in the weeks since she'd last seen her, Jennifer had changed. Something in her life had shifted.

Carol held out an apple. "You still eat these?"

Jennifer took it, bit. The crunch restored Carol. Hadn't she, at twenty, been confused? Hadn't she considered dropping out of college? Hadn't she pined over the wrong boys, done stupid things with her friends? All those concerns, all those missteps, meant nothing in the grand scheme of life. She could look back at that time with nostalgia now: how silly she had been, how simultaneously small and large the world had seemed, how sure she had been of her starring role. And how distant and rude she had been toward her mother. Much worse than Jennifer had ever been to her.

"I could use some money," Jennifer said, wiping her hands on her dress.

Carol got her purse out of the foyer closet. She wouldn't tell Drew—not about the money, not about this visit.

She had forty-eight dollars.

"That'll be enough for a couple weeks' groceries," she said.

Jennifer tucked the bills into her bag.

"Call me when you get home."

"I'm not going home now. I have—"

"An appointment. But call later. Let me know how whatever it is goes."

At the door, Jennifer spun around and hugged Carol, squeezing hard.

"I don't care if you skip the dinners," Carol said, patting her daughter's back, "but you have to come over and visit me."

"Deal," Jennifer said.

With a wave, she stepped inside the elevator. Carol watched the doors close.

Jennifer didn't call. Days passed, weeks.

And then late one afternoon, Carol spotted Jennifer in the subway, wearing the blue suede jacket, but Jennifer didn't hear Carol shout her name. And the next morning, when Carol called, Sandra answered Jennifer's phone, confused at first because she thought the phone was hers. Jennifer hadn't come back for it—no, she didn't know where Jennifer was.

Twenty-Two

On the 1 train, two teenage boys take over the center pole, performing gymnastics to a boom box's steady beat. The commuters allow them space but few turn their attention away from books and e-readers and cell phone screens. Those who do, smile; an older man claps along to the rhythm; feet tap. As the younger boy does a backflip, the older boy chants. Hey-ho. Hey-ho.

When the younger boy comes around with a baseball cap, Drew puts in a five-dollar bill. The kid reminds him of Ben, small for his age with that serious expression as if every action, no matter how slight, requires great concentration. He wonders if the two boys are brothers as they claim. They share little resemblance, but they could be half brothers, stepbrothers even, brothers by circumstance and association. Most likely their parents have no idea what they're up to.

He doesn't know how he is going to tell his son.

Twenty-Three

Carol thinks about decomposition, human flesh falling like boiled chicken from its bone. Her mother's body had looked like a stranger's in its casket, and that had been with the help of refrigeration, chemicals, a hairstylist, and a makeup artist. What had Drew seen? How could he be certain that whatever he saw was their daughter?

These are questions she cannot bring herself to ask, but she forces herself to envision a pile of bones, glowing white. She visualizes only one bone. Long and smooth. Made out of pearl.

Lying in bed on her stomach, she replays the video on her laptop. She tries to make out the one detail that will unravel all the rest, but she has seen it all, noticed everything. Seven seconds. Her daughter is there, and then gone. There, and then gone. There. Gone. The reversal of birth, of all Carol has given to this world—and for what?

For what?

Seven seconds.

Over the past year, she has thought about him.

She doesn't fantasize. She wouldn't use that word.

But despite herself, she respects him. He can't be anyone ordinary, lowbrow, mentally deficient. He's not a creature who crawled out of the shadows, snatched Jennifer, and crawled back in. No, he is a man of the world. Perceptive and intelligent, a smart dresser. He must have known what sort of task lay before him and been intrigued by the challenge. He would have had to rely on his charm, his finesse. A Ted Bundy type. A man who, in other circumstances, might have made an impressive husband.

She reaches for the moment Jennifer realized her mistake. She walked out willingly. Her head on his shoulder. Their arms linked. When they turned the corner, where did they go? His waiting car? His apartment a few blocks over? An alley, wedged into the space between the wall and the Dumpster?

Carol wants to look him in the eye. She wants to hear his voice. Smell his cologne. Feel the roughness or smoothness of his skin.

She wants to step into Jennifer's place, so that in that moment she can wrap her hands around his neck, like he did to Jennifer, and squeeze and squeeze until his eyes roll back in his head.

Twenty-Four

They have finished the beers and are smoking another bowl, their toes side by side on the coffee table, sandalwood incense mixing with the pot smoke, creating a cloud above their heads, when the door opens and a man comes in.

Ben knows who it is even before Sandra says his name. Trey is exactly as she described, except the movie star smile isn't there, only a deep frown.

"Helloooo?" the man says, and Ben dislikes him for the elongated syllable, as if he has a right to question Ben's presence. Ben flicks the lighter against the bowl, pretending everything is normal. *Kill them with confidence,* Jennifer used to tell him.

"This is Ben," Sandra says. "Jen's brother."

"What is this? Reunion day?"

Ben looks at the door, still ajar. Trey had a key.

"Close the door, stupid," Sandra says.

Trey nods to Ben. "Hey, man."

"Hey."

He hasn't shut the door. Sandra sighs dramatically. When she gets up, Ben's body falls into the empty space. Trey laughs, and there it is. Movie star. She shoves the door closed.

"Neighbors," she says, gesturing toward the bong cupped in Ben's hand.

"Sorry," Trey says. "Sorry, sorry." He flashes those dazzling teeth, those dimples at Ben, to commiserate, but Ben won't give him that. No matter what, no matter who has a key, he is on Sandra's side.

"We were trying to decide for the exhibit," Sandra says.

"So I see." Trey squats, forearms braced against his knees, and looks over the photographs. "Any progress?"

"Well," Sandra says. "I have an idea. See? The question mark can be the center point. And then all the solitary figures. It's like a collection of lost things."

Things. The word makes Ben feel off-balance. Dizzy. He puts the bong on the table and lies across the love seat, his feet hanging over the armrest.

"Lost and found," Trey says.

Ben rolls his eyes. A crack runs along the edge of the ceiling, and he follows it until it disappears into the wall.

"Yeah," Sandra says. "Sort of."

"And your collages?"

"The disembodied."

"Okay. I see where you're going. I like it."

"Ben thinks we should show all of them."

"Hey, man," Trey says, "if we had the wall space."

"Make the space," Ben says, trying to sound like he is in control, like he belongs here. He swings his legs over and sits up, but the dizziness overwhelms him, causes him to forget what he was going to say next.

"Uh-huh." Trey flashes his teeth at Sandra, but she has turned away, her back to Ben, so Ben cannot see her reaction.

"I understand your feelings," Trey says. "I honestly do. But the photos are going to stand out more if we just choose a few of them."

"What if you do another show later?" Ben says.

"Yeah," Trey says. "Maybe."

Sandra touches Trey's shoulder. "Tell him you'll do it."

"Okay, kid," Trey says, "I'll think about it, but not because you're telling me to. Your sister's photos fucking rock."

"I know," Ben says, noticing that Trey has switched from calling him *man* to calling him *kid*. When Sandra calls him *kid*, it's a term of endearment and he likes it. When Trey says *kid*, it's something else.

Trey hops up.

"Friday," he says, taking Sandra's hand and spinning her in a circle under his arm. "Friday, Friday. Is Friday still on?"

"No," Sandra says. "Didn't you hear? Friday's been repealed. New astrological order."

"Um."

"He's along for the ride."

Sandra disentangles her hand from Trey's and seems to float over to the love seat, resuming her place next to Ben. As she snuggles her shoulder against his, Ben looks right at Trey, staring him down.

"How old is he?" Trey says.

"Fifteen," Sandra says before Ben can say, "Old enough."

"Fifteen? Great."

"Why? What were you doing at fifteen?"

"That was me, not him."

"He's Jen's brother."

"Yeah, kid? What do you say? Can you party like your sister?"

"It doesn't have to be like that," Sandra says.

Trey's smile widens. "Consider tonight your coming-of-age story, kid."

Ben tries to think of a witty comeback, but his tongue lies heavy in his mouth, the top of his head lost within the hovering smoke.

Twenty-Five

Carol hears the apartment door open and holds still, as she used to as a child on mornings when she didn't want to go to school, as if by freezing her body, she could freeze time. Or move outside of it. She swallows hard, her body already betraying her with its need. Her name is being called, softly. She rolls over. Knocking on the bedroom door. She locked it, she remembers now. She is keeping herself safe.

But he won't go away, and she knows she can't expect him to. *I love you,* she thinks. *I hate you.* The word *hate* clenches her, every muscle a fist, poised for the fight. *I love you,* she tries again, but her body will not give an inch.

"Honey," he is saying. "Honey, please, open up."

She licks her lips. Her throat is dry. Next to her, on the laptop screen, the last moment of Jennifer's existence is frozen. Her daughter is about to turn the corner, but not yet. Not yet. Carol can still catch her if she hurries.

"Honey." Another tap. "Please."

He is getting in the way.

She should tell him this. She should tell him to go, to leave her alone. But as soon as the knocking stops, she misses it, his presence behind the door. She is afraid, suddenly, of the darkness in the room. She switches on the bedside lamp, pulls on her robe.

He is standing in the foyer, leaning against the credenza, arms folded, chin lowered to his chest. His shoes are muddy. She can smell his sweat from across the room.

He lifts his head, and she can tell that he has been crying but is finished now. He has saved his strongest self for her. And she will take it.

"I'm so sorry," he says, as if all of this is his fault, as if he could take it back, and opens his arms.

She falls against him, the surrender momentary but a relief. He holds up her weight, this man of strength. Of steel. He strokes the side of her head, his lips moving across her scalp, and it sounds like he's saying, "It's okay" or "We're okay," but that can't be right, because they aren't. They never will be again.

Twenty-Six

He will hold her forever, if that's what she wants. She is heavy against him, slack, and he wants to pick her up, carry her into the bedroom, but he doesn't know if she will allow it, where he is permitted to tread. He is cautious; there is only so much loss a person can take in a day. His lips move, but he doesn't know what he is saying. He just wants to make things better. Make everything all right. Do what she expects of him.

Stepping out of his embrace, she dries her face on her sleeve. She nods at her feet, looks up and nods at him. He doesn't know what it means.

"I'm going to lie down," she says.

"Where's Ben?"

She blinks slowly. "Out," she says. "With a friend." She pauses, trying to remember. "Mike."

"He needs to come home."

"Not yet."

"Carol—"

She holds up her hand. "Let him be."

"When is he supposed to be back?"

"Seven."

"It's six fifteen."

"So it's not seven. Let him be." She raises her chin, her eyes bright, defiant. "He's a good kid."

"I know he is."

"I hope you remember that."

Drew feels his heartbeat quicken. Are they really doing this right now? He wants to stop, but he can't help himself. He is being pushed into battle.

"What's that supposed to mean?" he says.

Carol lifts her shoulder in a half shrug. Her mouth opens and shuts, but she can't help herself either. "You pushed one away," she says. "Don't do it to the child we have left."

Drew grabs onto the credenza to keep from punching something—Carol, the wall. He has never felt the impulse to hit her before, and as soon as the flash is over, he hates himself for it. When he looks up, he is alone.

He stands outside their closed bedroom door and is transported back in time to when Jennifer was sixteen, the night she didn't come home. The way Carol swooped in the next day, becoming her confidant, pow-wowing behind Jennifer's bedroom door. Just like then, he has been shut out, despised.

He places his hand against the door. Holds it there. But he will not knock. He has used up his strength already; he has none left to beg.

In the kitchen, he opens the dusty bottle of scotch, pours. He carries his drink into the living room. On the way, he sees his suit jacket slung across the credenza in the foyer. The carelessness bothers him. He hangs the jacket up in the hall closet and takes out the notebook, lays it on the coffee table.

He has been writing for Jennifer; there is no point in continuing. He should throw the notebook away, but there's still so much to tell her, so much he hasn't gotten to, so many things yet to explain.

He roots around the side-table drawer for a pen.

Your mom and Ben were asleep. You were coming out of the bathroom, I was coming out of my bedroom, and we both stopped. It was never just the two of us but there we were, alone and facing each other down in the hall. I'm not sure which one of us smiled first. But there, in your eyes, I saw it—respect. An acknowledgment of our mutual stubbornness. I felt it too and hoped you understood. I could have told you the story of when I was sixteen and my buddies and I took off for Canada for the weekend. We decided after school on a Friday and took off in Donnie's brother's car. No cell phones back then. Our parents were livid, and we didn't even do much: just drove around, drank beer in a cheap motel room, tried and failed to score with Canuck girls, but it was one of the best weekends of my life. I'd forgotten about it until just then. I'd never told anyone, not even your mom, but I should have told you.

We were alike in more ways than I was comfortable admitting.

"Morning, pumpkinseed," I said.

I hadn't called you that in years. You got it, I saw the way your face opened before it clenched shut. You glared at me as you passed, but you closed your door softly. You didn't slam it.

I'm not sure what I would have done if you'd said good morning in return. Maybe we could have gone into the kitchen and shared some milk, a late night snack. Maybe that's only something fathers and daughters do on TV. Bonding.

*I wanted to raise you and Ben to be strong, good peo-
ple. I wanted your life to unfold without adversity. I didn't
want you to end up pregnant or a dropout or addicted to
drugs or dead. Those aren't great demands. Most of all I
never wanted you to be disappointed. And so maybe I was
a little too hard. A little too rigid. Judgmental. I didn't
know any other way to be. That's how my dad raised me,
and I don't think I turned out so bad.*

*I am the one who went to claim you. No one else
could do that. Not your mom, not those friends of yours.
Only me. I hope you understand what that means. How
much I have always loved you. How you've always been
your father's daughter, even when I wished you weren't
(I'm sorry).*

Twenty-Seven

They pull the curtain, as if that will prevent Ben from hearing. He shuts his eyes to relieve the spinning of the room and concentrate on their voices. He shouldn't have smoked the second bowl; he shouldn't have had that beer. If he were to throw up now, it would be beyond embarrassing, proof of his childishness, his uncool. Worthy of expulsion.

He scrunches into the love seat. The cushions are so soft, they conform to his body, and the movement in his head stills. His hearing amplifies. A sudden super-skill.

"I'm not planning on babysitting," Trey says.

"It's not *babysitting*. He's cool."

"This a regular thing? The two of you hanging out?"

"Does it bother you?"

"It's just a little strange. Jen's relatives traipsing in and out."

"I like the kid."

Ben's lips move, repeating the kiss. He is sure—absolutely positive—she kissed him back.

"He's not Jen."

"Of course he's not Jen. But he needs me—it's just nice having him around, okay?"

"This is a guilt thing, Sand."

"It is *not* a guilt thing."

The metal stud sliding along his tongue, clicking against his teeth.

"What do *you* need?"

"I need you to fuck off. Stop pretending like you care. You're just pissed because you think he's going to ruin your night."

The raised voices are a good sign. Trey will leave now. He will burst through the curtain and out the door, tossing the key behind him.

"Okay," Trey says. "Okay."

"And it won't be like that."

"That kid freaks out, you take him home. Or you put his ass in a cab."

"Trust me on this, all right?"

Lips smacking against lips. Ben squirms. He opens his eyes to make his hearing powers go away. The yellow curtain pulls back. Sandra and Trey have both changed clothes: she into a short, tight dress, electric blue, with thigh-high boots the same color; he, a black mesh top beneath a denim jacket. They look good together. Like a couple. The dragon tattoo around Trey's neck is kind of awesome, Ben has to admit.

He looks down at his T-shirt and cargo shorts. He doesn't own anything cooler than this. At least his T-shirt is black.

"Hungry?" Sandra says, pressing her hands against her stomach. "I'm starved. Should we pop open a can of beans?"

"Those are provisions," Ben says.

"Kidding! I'm kidding."

"Provisions for what?" Trey asks.

"The world's ending," Sandra says. "Didn't you hear?"

"Is this like that Mayan prophecy shit?"

"It's science," Ben says. "Global warming. It's changing the earth's patterns, raising sea levels, increasing storms. Hurricane Sandy—"

"Hurricane Sandy sucked," Trey says. "I had to go stay with my parents for a week."

"Oh, boohoo," Sandra says. "What Ben's talking about will be a hundred times worse. Look, he got me this, too."

She picks up the duct tape off the counter, waves it in Trey's face. Trey grabs the tape and pulls her wrists behind her back.

"Maybe we'll have fun with this later," he says.

Ben's disgusted, but Sandra laughs as she wiggles free. She plucks the tape out of Trey's hand.

"You are an idiot," she says. "It's for the windows, right, Ben? To reinforce the glass. Ben's going to keep me safe."

"What'll happen to me?"

"You'll drown," Ben says.

Sandra puts the tape back on the counter.

"You don't pack a gun," Trey says. "Do you?"

"I'm not into violence."

"But you're okay with telling me I'll drown?"

"I'm just stating the facts."

"What about when food runs short? Aren't you supposed to have, like, a stockpile of weapons to defend against the marauding crowds?"

"Our food won't run short. Not for a long time. We'll be prepared, and we'll help anyone else who prepared." Ben knows he is in the minority in this belief—that at the End, those who have survived will come together and work as one instead of fighting and killing each other. Of course there will be people who commit violence, just as there are now, but evil is the exception to the rule—there are more people like Jennifer than like the person who took her; for his own sanity, he has to believe this. Most people will be good and do good and help those in need, Ben and Sandra included.

"You have an interesting philosophy, kid," Trey says. "I'm not saying I agree with you, but it's interesting. I might be banging on your door one of these days."

"We won't let you in," Sandra says and grins at Ben, her tongue poking out between her teeth.

"I like your dress," Ben says.

She claps her hands. "Food!"

As if on command, Ben's stomach growls. He hasn't eaten since the pancakes that morning. The thought of the whipped cream makes his mouth water.

"Indian?" Trey says.

"We had that last night," Sandra says.

Trey looks from Sandra to Ben and back.

"There's whole worlds here," he says, wrapping his arms around Sandra from behind.

She sidesteps out of Trey's embrace. Ben thinks she's on her way to him, but she plops down on the papasan.

"Look at those," she says quietly, gazing down at Jennifer's photographs.

She reaches behind her for Trey's hand.

"Thank you," she says, head tilted back to look at him. "I mean that. We both do."

The back-and-forth confuses Ben: Sandra's and Trey's bodies connecting and disconnecting, attracting one moment and repelling the next. Trey has a key. But Sandra kissed Ben. She let Ben kiss her, and she didn't pull away. Not immediately. Her lips parted, and her tongue sought his, and he felt the stud. He's kissed only one other girl, Jessie Levine, in seventh grade. And Taylor Poindexter, but he won't count her. They were eight or nine and just playing around on a class trip to the Bronx Zoo. Jessie was real; he guesses he could have called her his girlfriend, his first girlfriend, except they never went out on a date, just sat together at lunch for a couple months before she changed her mind and decided to sit with her friends again. He didn't care. He found her kind of boring.

But kissing Sandra—that meant something.

"I know," Sandra says. *"Cubano."*

Twenty-Eight

Carol fills the bathtub. When steam rises, she adds five drops of rose oil to the water. The rose oil is in a little amber glass bottle, recovered from Jennifer's medicine cabinet along with partial bottles of Tylenol and Ambien, a box of Band-Aids, a packet of birth control pills (Jennifer had been at the beginning of her cycle), a near-empty jar of Lotil skin cream that Carol had bought her two winters before. Drew pitched the Lotil, along with the Ambien and birth control, but the Tylenol and Band-Aids blended in on their shelf. The Tylenol has been used up, the bottle tossed by Drew, but the Band-Aids remain, incognito.

As she slides into the water, Carol inhales deeply. She stretches out her arms and legs and thinks about Jennifer, about the others, about the hundreds, thousands, of lost girls. Behind her closed eyelids, they are a collage of high school graduation photos: wide eyes, long lashes, white teeth, red lips, sun-kissed skin covering fortified muscles and bones.

When she meets him, the echo of Jennifer's heart will beat faster.

"Tell me everything," she'll say.

Or "Take me there."

Or nothing at all.

She won't have to.

At the age of twenty-four, three months into her new life in New York City, Carol met Drew at a party thrown by a friend of a friend in a Midtown tower, the lights of Manhattan glittering below. The view captivated Carol, and scared her a little, the order wrong, as if she were looking at the night sky in reverse. In the real sky above, no stars shone, a contrast to the sparkling expanses of her childhood, the constellations hardly a puzzle as she lay on her back in the field behind her house or meandered tipsily across the baseball diamond with her friends in the little town where she went to college. Here, the sky barely existed. Everything of importance went on below.

She stayed by the window while the party churned behind her. Voices created a frenzied overcurrent to Eurythmics on the stereo. A woman shrieked in laughter. A glass broke. Carol's friend had disappeared soon after they'd arrived, gone in search of an ex-boyfriend rumored to be in attendance. So far Carol's friend was her only one in the city, and she couldn't even be sure that's what they were to each other. They worked together as assistants to Thomas Merchile, an up-and-coming interior designer whose sadistic side showed itself in the way he pitted the two women against each other, favoring one on Monday, the other on Tuesday, neither on Wednesday. Sometimes the "friend" would commiserate; sometimes she wouldn't speak to Carol for days at a time, communicating only through notes. Carol daydreamed about quitting. It would take another year before she did.

"If you crane your neck, you can see Times Square."

Carol felt a hand on the small of her back. She flinched, and the hand fell away. Grinning, the man looked down into his drink. He had a pudgy face, curly brown hair a little too long. Like the rest of the men, he wore a polo shirt and jeans.

"That way," he said, pointing to the right.

Carol leaned toward the glass. Over there, Times Square throbbed like a casino.

"My name's Drew, by the way."

She took his hand, chilled from his drink.

"Carol."

"You like the view?"

"It's spectacular," she said, with more intensity than she'd intended.

"I've seen better," Drew said.

"Where's that?"

"Empire State Building."

That made her laugh.

"You haven't been up?" he said.

"I'm new here."

"That's the first thing all the tourists do—stand in line for three hours, go up, and take a roll of pictures."

"I'm not a tourist. I'm just new."

"Well," Drew said, "we'll have to remedy that."

The *we* struck her as presumptuous, and she didn't know what they were supposed to remedy—her newness or not being a tourist or never having been up the Empire State Building. She mentally chided herself for being so critical. Since moving to New York, she'd pulled inward instead of radiating out as she had hoped, in danger of becoming a recluse, of running back home, where her parents wouldn't say a word, their silence conveying their "I told you so."

"What are you drinking?" Drew asked.

"Riesling."

As Carol watched him walk toward the kitchen, she wrapped her arms around her torso, her hands clawing her ribs through the dress she'd bought in the hopes of someday going to a party like this one. Her

LBD, with tasteful three-inch heels to match. Her imagined New York life played through her head: the sophisticated wardrobe, the bright Chelsea apartment with the hardwood floors and skylights, the interior design job that challenged her, the boss who saw her promise and lauded her, the group of artistic friends who appreciated her uniqueness and invited her out to dinners at funky Village hot spots and to parties at apartments like this one. Instead she color-coded swatches and made lunch reservations, getting paid barely enough to cover her rent. She lived in a dark Washington Heights apartment with roommates she didn't see for days on end, and every time she rode the subway, she felt afraid.

So far this party was the only one of her visions that had come true, and here she was, distancing herself from its center, focusing on the view so she wouldn't have to deal with her sense of being in entirely the wrong place, of being entirely the wrong person.

When Drew returned, he did not touch the small of her back. He held out a plastic wine goblet, generously filled.

"Thank you," she said and made a point of meeting and holding his eyes, noting the color: blue. She'd always liked guys with blue eyes.

"How do you know Steven?" he asked.

"Who?"

"The guy whose living room we're standing in."

"Oh. My friend Charlene. Well, we're coworkers. I guess they went to school together or something."

"Charlene," Drew said. "I don't think I've met her."

"Big hair." Carol waved her hand above her head to approximate the size of Charlene's perm. "Pretty. Wears a lot of eye shadow."

"Sounds memorable, but I don't remember."

"What about you? How do you know Steven?"

"We work for the same fund." He saw Carol's confusion.

"Investments," he said.

They spent the rest of the night at the window. She discovered nothing extraordinary about Drew; he did not impress her with his looks or charm or wit. But he made her feel safe. He paid attention. The noise of the party receded as one question and answer led to the next, and she realized how simple this new life of hers could be. All she had to do was follow his lead, and he opened her up, freed her from the fantasies in her head and delivered her into the comforts of mundanity, of trust.

As the party wound down, they exchanged numbers. He hailed her a cab and pecked her on the cheek like a gentleman before sending her off into the night.

He called two days later, and that Friday he took her to dinner at an Italian restaurant that seemed plucked out of a movie, from the candles in Chianti bottles to the signed photographs of opera singers on the walls to the waiter's accented English. Drew asked what she wanted, and when she didn't know, overwhelmed by the variety of pastas, he ordered for them both. The ravioli melted in her mouth. She drank and drank as if the wine were water, and as she drank, she allowed herself to fall in love with him, because she wanted to keep having meals like this one. She'd stepped into a new New York fantasy: attainable. Their own.

The next weekend, after sushi, he took her back to his apartment, a few blocks over from Steven's but with a view of a brick wall, and made love to her on his futon. The sex wasn't mind-blowing, but she hadn't expected it to be. Their bodies moved in a comfortable rhythm, as if they were already married, and when she woke the next morning, he had made them coffee, which they drank while reading the *Times*.

Carol had been lucky. That night at the party could have turned out very differently if another man had approached and placed his hand confidently against the small of her back. She was eager to be saved. To be stolen away. Drew could have slipped a pill or powder into her drink. He could have gotten into the cab beside her. Once in his apartment, he could have bolted the door. He could have pinned her down. Wrapped his hands around her throat.

She read only two or three newspaper articles about Jennifer, just scanning—eyes following the lines but taking nothing in. Morton had told her not to read them, not to listen to the radio or TV, and she had tried not to. She let Drew deal with the reporters, but she heard his clipped tone, saw the stern look in his eyes. She imagined the questions, the accusations. A young woman leaving a bar with a strange man. Shouldn't Jennifer have understood the dangers, known better? Without a suspect, the people's blame had to go somewhere, so that they could feel protected.

Slut-shaming, Sandra once said, and Carol bridled at the word *slut* until Sandra explained that the word itself wasn't bad, only the way people have used it.

Carol understands—she is no different from Jennifer, from the others. She could have been one of those girls. She is one of those girls, and so she will never condemn them. She will never ask them why.

Twenty-Nine

In the living room Drew nurses his drink. The clock on the bookcase is an heirloom from Carol's family, a small wooden box outlined in spotted brass, brought over in some ancestor's suitcase from Germany. The minute hand jerks. Seven o'clock comes and goes. He puts his drink down, listens. The apartment has never seemed so quiet.

Seven ten. Seven fifteen. Seven twenty.

He goes to the foyer, faces the apartment door.

This is who Drew is, the person his family has made him: a man of action. Straitlaced. A straight shooter.

A man who, when called upon, does what he has to do. Claims the decaying remains of a Jane Doe dumped in a cave as his own flesh and blood. Would gather that body in his arms and carry it home if they would let him, lay it in bed, cover it with a blanket, read it a story, thinking about that blond hair, matted with mud, being clean from last night's bath and smelling of baby shampoo.

Carol, he is sure, wishes him dead in Jennifer's place. And he would go, if he had the option. If he could make that trade. But he can't.

What choice has he been given but to stay alive, their expectations piled onto his back, weighing him down so that day after day he crawls through the apartment, crawls down the street, belly scraping the pavement, crawls through the filth of the subway, crawls across the marble lobby and into the elevator, up seventeen floors, to prop himself up behind a desk, toss fake money into a game of hit-or-miss, keep the system running, bring home a paycheck, do what he is supposed to do, be a father, be a husband, be a man?

Provide, so that his wife can slip out in the middle of the night and fuck another man, different men. So his son can carouse the streets of New York untethered, naïve. So that his daughter can be stolen, dead.

How can this be his life?

Drew does not try his bedroom door; he has no need for his wife, not now.

For the second time today, he goes to his son's room. He is justified; he pays for these walls. But Ben's room feels like a foreign country, Drew the invader. Jennifer's room he understood: the clothes strewn over the floor, the posters taped to the walls (he'd scolded her, as his father had him—tape ruins paint), the bed unmade, and books and papers and photographs and strange, secret knickknacks (bottle caps, dried roses, postcards for parties she was too young to attend, brightly colored wristbands snipped off) thrown about as if an explosion had occurred. Jennifer, bursting from the seams. He had been her once: growing, becoming, feeling as if New York, this world, were too small to contain something so great—the possibility of everything.

But Ben's room—Ben's room shows nothing but restraint. A soul packed down to nonexistence. Drew sits on the bed and plucks at the hospital corners. Do Ben's skinny arms strain, trying to get the sheet over the mattress, just so?

He opens Ben's desk drawer, hopeful for a clue to give him a sense of direction. Computer paper on the left, extra ink cartridges in the middle, a dictionary on the right. Who uses a physical dictionary anymore? He opens it, flips through the musty pages. It's Carol's old dictionary from college. There, inside the front cover, is her name in careful, looping script, a more elegant version of her chicken scratch.

Underneath, Drew finds a magazine: *Urban Survivalist*. The cover shows a woman with a shaved head wearing fatigues, carrying a semi-automatic, a city burning behind her.

A sick feeling unpeels in Drew's stomach, a slick mixture of embarrassment and dread, as if he has come across Ben's porn stash. The woman is not unattractive, her breasts ample and glistening inside her camouflage bra. Inside the magazine, advertisements for modular bunkers. How to pack a bugout bag. The worst city to occupy: New York, of course. If you must stay, what to do. The probability of natural disaster, foreign attack, nuclear war conveyed in graphs to give the semblance of science. Crap.

Drew tosses the magazine back in the drawer and leaves it open, the dictionary on the bed, so Ben will know what he has seen. He opens Ben's laptop, but the kid has it password protected. The background image is a close-up of Ben and Jennifer, grinning.

Ben's cell phone goes to voice mail.

"Ben, it's Dad. Call me back. We need to talk to you. It's . . . it's getting late, and your mom—she's getting worried. Time to come home, bud."

Thirty

"Jennifer loved this place," Sandra says, and that's all she needs to say for Ben to appreciate the starkness of the restaurant, the tile floors and tile walls like the cafeteria at school. Sandra slides into the booth first, and Ben moves fast, sliding in behind her so Trey has to sit across. Right away he doubts his decision; he gets to feel Sandra beside him, but she's looking at Trey. They eat all together off one big plate. The rice and beans don't taste like anything special, but he guesses it's like the coffee and beer, another acquired taste. He's trying, and with each bite, it gets tastier. There's coffee, too, in Styrofoam cups. There's no waitress offering refills, so he takes his time. "Eat up," Sandra says. "You'll need your energy. We are going to go all night." And Trey starts singing "All Night Long" in a high falsetto until Sandra stabs his hand with her fork. Outside the streets fill up. The people look good; they have their going-out clothes on. Cars clog Delancey Street. Light leaks from the sky, bleeding off the edges, and the coffee is doing its trick; Ben can feel it flooding his veins, giving him strength. He's feeling good, he can do this. He's ready to go all night.

Thirty-One

"Carol," Drew says through the door. "Where's your address book? I need to find Ben."

She gets up, reties her bathrobe.

Ben.

Ben.

Where is Ben?

"Did you hear me?" Drew says.

"He isn't home?"

"No."

She grips the doorknob, unsure whether to undo the lock or add her weight to it.

"What's his friend's name again?" Drew says.

"Mike."

"Do you have his number?"

She should—but she doesn't.

"The address book," Drew says.

"In the credenza. I think. Did you call Ben?"

"He's not answering." Drew pauses. "I'm sure he's fine."

"Yes."

"He should be here."

"Yes."

"I might have to go look for him. Will you be all right? If I go?"

"Please," she says. "Go."

She feels the doorknob turn, stop.

"I love you," Carol says.

For a long moment, he says nothing.

"I love you, too."

She listens, but she can't tell if he's moved away. She slumps against the wall, pressing her forehead against the door.

I love you, love you, love you.

But I love her more.

Tonight Carol will turn the tables; she will do this one last thing—the most important thing—for her little girl.

The cross earrings are tarnished. She rubs them with a piece of toilet paper, but it does nothing. No matter—he won't be able to tell in the dark.

She slips the ladybug charm onto a silver chain, fastens it around her neck, imagining the charm dangling from a bracelet on Delia's slender wrist, remembering the jangle of her own bracelet, the joy the sound would bring.

Tonight, for Jennifer—for all the girls—she won't allow herself to fail.

Thirty-Two

"We still on?" Trey says, and Sandra says, "Hook us up."

Trey leads the way. They walk single file, Ben in the rear, his eyes lowered to take in Sandra's electric-blue hips. He hears the click of her heels above the chatter of passersby, the beeping of a truck backing up and hurtling down the street, the ambient buzz of the city. Even walking, she seems to be dancing. He has imagined her at his age, a ballerina in Nebraska, stuffing her toe shoes in her locker for dance class after school. She was lonely in Nebraska; dance saved her, although she has never said from what. After high school she bought a one-way Greyhound ticket, arriving in New York with nowhere to live, without knowing a soul. Ben didn't think anyone did that except in movies, but she did. Within a week, she fell down a flight of stairs and messed up her back. "Fucking subway stairs," she said. "Everyone stepped over me. That's why I don't like to leave home before noon. PTSD from the morning commute." Ben can't see anything wrong with her back, any stiffness or soreness in the way she moves. The way she flows. But there's something enticing about the tragic flaw beneath her skin, embedded deep within her muscle. At any time the old injury could flare up, and he could be called upon to place his hands where she needs them and ease away the pain.

His head is clearer now, thanks to the rice and beans and coffee and cool evening air, but there's still a blur around the edges, a softening. It feels nice. He touches Sandra's elbow, and she looks over her shoulder, distracted, her mouth forming words. He hadn't realized she was talking. Trey says something back, but whatever it is, is lost.

"What?" Ben says, but Sandra turns away. They are walking fast, on a mission. Ben remembers the lock he hasn't put on his room. It's still in the paper bag on Sandra's kitchen counter, but he doubts his dad will go back in tonight—Ben doesn't remain on his dad's mind for very long. Still, tomorrow morning, first thing, the lock goes on.

They pass beneath a flowering tree, one of the first of the season. Ben reaches up and captures white petals in his hand. He pours them over Sandra, and she laughs, shaking her head. The petals stay, glowing against her dark hair.

How did they get here, to the store with the dead animals?

Trey is knocking on the door with Sandra close behind, her hand on Trey's back, pressing him forward.

"Wait," Ben says. He points at the window, at a loss for words.

"Yeah," Sandra says. "Creepy, right?"

Nothing in the window has changed, but the bones seem more vulnerable now, exposed, like the people in Jennifer's photographs—anyone can walk by, anyone can see. It has been that way all along. He wonders why he didn't recognize it before.

Impossibly, there is someone moving toward them through the store's darkness.

The door opens, and Trey goes in, followed by Sandra, who grabs Ben's wrist, pulling him along.

The man towers over them, so tall that he seems to stoop beneath the low ceiling. He has the palest skin Ben has ever seen and shaggy white-blond hair, his sinewy arms covered in ink.

"Duncan," Sandra says. "This is Ben."

"What's up?" Duncan gives Ben a nod as he clicks the dead bolt into place. Trey is already in the back, going through an arched doorway. Music is playing, an odd mix, tribal sounding, drums and chanting male and female voices.

"Jen's brother," Sandra says.

"Yeah?" Duncan gives Ben a closer look, his eyes a startling, washed-out blue. "Jen's brother. Wow."

"Hi," Ben says.

"Is this your circle?" Sandra asks.

"Yep." Duncan places his hands on his hips. "From Saturday."

Sandra cocks her head. It takes Ben a second to realize that they're listening to the music.

"Pretty cool, huh?" Duncan says.

"*Very* cool," Sandra says.

Duncan blushes—it's a dramatic effect on someone so light. *Gentle giant,* Ben thinks. Like Lurch from *The Addams Family.*

Already he likes Duncan much better than Trey.

To their left is a counter, the display cabinet below full of fossils of various sizes, chunks of amber as large as fists, a lizard skeleton three feet long, another, smaller cow's skull. The place has the solemn feel of a museum or gallery, but nothing is marked with a description, nothing has a price.

"Ben likes your pets," Sandra says, and Duncan laughs.

The back room is jungle, forest, warehouse, and bedroom squeezed into a space smaller than Ben's kitchen. On a beaten-up leather couch, Trey sits with his feet propped on a cardboard box, opposite a cot pushed up against the wall. He has slung his jacket over the outstretched arms of a grizzly bear. Above the bed a lion's head mutely roars.

"Best taxidermist in the city," Sandra says as Ben touches the spread wing of a falcon, the feathers surprisingly soft.

"He's the shit," Trey says.

Duncan shrugs. "I don't like to see dead things go to waste. Especially when they're beautiful."

"What've you got for us?" Trey says, sitting up, rubbing his hands together.

Duncan swings the lion's head to the side, revealing a metal shelf, and takes down a cigar box.

"Fresh from Montreal," he says.

"Not that heroin-laced shit," Trey says. "That stuff knocked me out."

"Pure." Duncan shakes a little plastic bag full of white pills. Trey holds out his hand, and Duncan drops the bag onto his palm.

Sandra steps close to Ben. "You're down for this?" she says, keeping her voice low.

Ben nods, although he isn't sure what the pills are, what he's agreeing to.

"You've done it before?" she says.

"What?"

"MDMA." She looks hard into his face.

"Sure," Ben says.

"It's not chill, not like pot . . ."

"Yeah, I know."

Sandra plucks a petal from her hair and puts it on Ben's head. "You're my partner in crime, huh?" she says.

"You bet."

Trey stands, stuffing the plastic bag into his pocket. He bares his teeth at the bear and growls. Duncan growls back, and Trey jumps on one foot, hands in the air.

"We'll see you later?" Sandra says.

"Nope." Duncan replaces the box on the shelf. "Working tonight."

"Lion, tiger, or bear?"

"Some old lady's labradoodle. Her kids want it for her birthday tomorrow."

"That's sick," Trey says.

"It's a surprise."

"God," Sandra says. "Hope she doesn't have a heart attack."

Duncan goes with them into the front room. At the door, he shakes Ben's hand.

"Good to meet you, Jen's brother," he says.

"Thanks." Looking into Duncan's pale eyes, Ben wants to know more—about his relationship with Jennifer and the beautiful dead things, whether Jennifer touched the falcon's silky feathers, if some afternoon Ben can knock on the door and be let inside. But Sandra and Trey have already stepped out, and all he can manage is "You, too."

"Fight the good fight," Duncan says and locks the door behind them.

Dusk has slipped into night, and they have this stretch of Orchard Street to themselves. Sandra links one arm through Trey's, the other through Ben's as they pass gated shops, shadows of leather jackets and fur coats in the windows, a sharp contrast to Duncan's undead dead, lovingly preserved. Ben has never had much of an opinion on leather and fur, but now he decides never to wear either again.

"New moon," Sandra says, and the night does seem darker than most, but when Ben looks up, he sees no stars, only the reflection of city lights. He remembers going to visit his grandparents in Ohio, the sky above their farmhouse so crowded with constellations that it terrified him. His grandpa gave Jennifer a picture book, and she tried to point out the shapes. Ben followed her finger, but the stars seemed to multiply before his eyes.

"The sun is a star," she read to him, but it was too much for either of them to fathom.

Here, there is nothing man has not made. A human space carved out in the universe with brutal force, the cause of its own destruction.

A space where man can bring the dead back to life.

It's a tenuous security, but for now he'll take it. He'll take it tonight with the pressure of Sandra's arm through his, the white petals in her hair, the white pills in Trey's pocket, the rhythm of their feet falling together, echoing back to them off pavement and brick and into the new-moon night, an army of three.

Thirty-Three

Carol's address book is where she said it would be, in the credenza, beneath the phone. As Drew flips through the book—numbers and addresses crossed out, rewritten in the margins in Carol's chicken scratch, whole sections x-ed—he wonders how many years have passed since Carol used this thing. There's the kids' former pediatrician and the dentist who passed away. The high school girl who used to babysit and probably now has children of her own. The Silversteins. When did they last speak to the Silversteins?

Even as he searches, he acknowledges the futility—no friend of Ben's would be listed in here, not by first name, anyway. Almost all the names are women, mothers. Markings on the side, some sort of code. Check marks. Initials. Stars. Question marks.

Under *R* he finds Julie Rothchild. Carol used to spend a lot of time with her, talk about her incessantly, but months have passed since he last heard her name. Julie has a daughter in Ben's grade. Drew dials, fully expecting a stranger to tell him he has the wrong number, but Julie answers in the warm voice he remembers now, and the face comes back to him, her small features and energetic brown eyes, pretty and peppy like an aged cheerleader.

"Drew," Julie says. "How are you?"

The question is so simple, rudimentary politeness, and yet it takes his breath away. He wants to answer honestly, tell her everything. Unburden himself. He presses a hand against the wall; the action steadies him.

"I'm looking for Ben," he says. "He told Carol he was spending the day with a friend named Mike. No last name. I thought maybe you'd know who it was."

"Mike. I'm not sure. There are a few different Mikes. Hang on."

She reads names and numbers off a list from the school. Carol used to have lists like that, limbs on the phone tree secured to the refrigerator with an apple-shaped magnet from the PTO. The names mean nothing to Drew. He writes them down dutifully, although his heart sinks with each addition. Five Mikes. In age-old tradition, each one likely categorized in the classroom by his last initial: Mike H., Mike R., two Mike M.'s, Mike P. Drew sets the pen down, certain Ben is not with any of them.

"It was good to see Carol today," Julie says.

"You saw Carol?"

"Didn't she tell you? She came by this afternoon. I needed her professional opinion on a couple of chairs. But, Drew." Julie lowers her voice. "She isn't coping well, is she?"

"I identified the body today," Drew says.

A relief, to say it out loud, to someone who is nearly a stranger. If Carol won't go to Dr. Rubin, maybe Drew should. Maybe he should have kept that pamphlet from the preschool teacher instead of wadding it up, tossing it into the trash in Battery Park. He imagines calling up the hotline and letting whoever is on the other end carry his pain for a while.

"The body?" Julie says.

"Jennifer's body."

"My God. Drew."

"Yes," Drew says, staring at his hand flat against the wall. "That happened."

"I'm so sorry. Are you—do you need anything?"

"Right now I just need to find Ben."

"Yes. Of course. Does he know?"

"No, not yet."

"Drew. My God." Julie's voice breaks, and Drew holds the phone away from his ear until she pulls herself back together.

"Let me check up on the Mikes," she says.

"You don't need to do that."

"Please, let me call them. It's the very least I can do, and I'd like to do something."

While he waits for Julie to call back, he searches Ben's room. Porn, at least, he could understand. A *Playboy* would be a starting point, and Drew would be cool. He'd bring it up casually, or never mention it at all, just put the magazine back in the drawer, the dictionary on top, maybe a pack of condoms thrown in. He'd look at his son a little differently, this perfectly normal secret between them, a sign of his son's appropriately blossoming private life.

Survivalist brings to mind stockpiled guns and ammunition, bunkers in the desert, years' worth of canned goods and freeze-dried military meals. It's the woman with the butt-long braid and ankle-length denim skirt handing out end-of-the-world pamphlets in Grand Central. It's the chubby guy in stained fatigues marching up and down Seventy-Second Street holding the American flag on a broom handle. It's the rambling commentators on Fox News. Not reasonable, not *good*, not like Ben.

He starts with the desk because there are only so many places to hide things, but there is nothing beneath the computer paper, no more magazines secreted away. When he opens the dresser drawers, he finds

Ben's clothes arranged by type: top drawer boxers and balled socks; middle drawer T-shirts, long-sleeved shirts, and sweatshirts in three neat stacks; bottom drawer shorts, sweatpants, jeans. Where once Drew saw dullness, now he sees an eviscerating trait, hints of an obsessive personality, primness. He jerks out the middle drawer and dumps the contents on the bed, standing over the mess as if the clothes might reorder themselves into some type of message.

He sits on the floor, his back against the bed. His legs and arms ache from the afternoon's run. He got mud all over his shoes, although he doesn't know how, doesn't remember straying from the paths. Tomorrow he will clean them. The thought of half an hour with polish and an old rag gives him comfort. Just like his father, newspapers spread out on the floor, setting things right with the strength of his wrists.

Ben's nightstand used to be the telephone stand in Drew's parents' house, and he experiences a moment of déjà vu, sitting on the floor like this, back against the wall, staring at the oak grain in the silence after a failed conversation with Tracey Bender or Gina Orsatti.

Drew had been a good kid, too, despite all the times he and his father had butted heads, despite his mother's declarations that he'd better watch it, he was on a one-way ticket to hell. Both only children, Drew and Carol wanted two, so that neither child would have to bear the brunt of their parents alone. There were miscarriages—three, maybe four—between Jennifer and Ben, and for a while it looked like Jennifer would be all they had. They never admitted as much to each other, but they grew accustomed to the idea. Drew forgot that, technically, they were still trying, and when the pregnancy stayed, it was a surprise, a shock, really. Just like that, their family of three turned into a family of four.

And now—what are they? A family of what?

He opens the cupboard at the base of the nightstand. There is nothing inside but a cheap saint candle, like the ones in Sandra's apartment. Saint Anthony, cradling baby Jesus in his arms.

On the opposite side, he finds the prayer:

Saint Anthony, perfect imitator of Jesus, who received from God the special power of restoring lost things, grant that I may find (mention your petition) which has been lost. At least restore to me peace and tranquility of mind, the loss of which has afflicted me even more than my material loss.

Thirty-Four

Ben's phone vibrates. He slips it out of his pocket and looks at the screen.

His dad.

Shit.

Ben should have put the lock on his door.

That morning his dad had looked panicked, wild, standing in the middle of his room. When he saw Ben in the doorway, his expression changed to disappointment. "Wipe your lip," he said, squeezing past, and the way he said it, with disregard, disdain, made Ben shrink. He went into the bathroom, and there was a smear of cream cheese on his upper lip. Childish. He wiped his mouth, washed his whole face.

His phone stops vibrating. The voice mail icon appears.

It's almost ten. His dad should be in bed. Ben doesn't know about his mom. Last night he saw her leave. He was in the kitchen, getting a drink of water, when he heard movement in the foyer. She was dressed in clothes that weren't her style, not like the person she used to be, anyway—more like Jennifer. He watched her step into the hall. He almost called out to her but didn't.

Sandra reaches back, wiggles her fingers.

Ben puts his phone away and jogs up to take her hand.

Thirty-Five

Not waiting for Julie's call, he runs out of the apartment, down the stairs, two at a time, bursts through the lobby, hears "In a hurry, Mr. Bauer?" as the doors slam open, shut, runs out into the night, down the block, each footstep vibrating, the night vibrating, his arm outstretched, an antenna straining for signals, receiving none, reaching toward Broadway, reaching for a cab, "The fastest way," he tells the cabbie, and this is what the cabbie's been waiting for, a chance to show off his skills, peeling off into traffic, whiplashing through lanes, every light green, but Drew doesn't look at what's going on out there; he concentrates on the cracked upholstery, seeing her ferrety face, his son enfolded in those bird arms, inside that tattered green kimono, against that breast stabbed through with a ring like a bull's nose, and she's laughing with her head thrown back, her eyes rolled back; he sees the red at the back of her throat, because she has what she wants—she's stealing his family one by one.

Thirty-Six

Two months had passed since Jennifer disappeared. They needed to clear out the apartment. The police had no more need of it, and while the woman who sublet to Jennifer had been generous, now she had to fill the space, collect rent. Couldn't they pay? Carol asked, and Drew said no, no. No.

Together they piled clothes on the bed, into trash bags to cart off to Housing Works. He could take only the morning off and left her alone around lunchtime. She called Sandra.

"Take whatever you want. She loved you. You should have her . . . things."

She watched Sandra's arms fill with a rainbow of shirts and dresses and scarves.

Sandra held up a skirt to Carol. "I can't wear this," Sandra said. "She was so much taller than me."

"It would never fit."

"Take it. And this. This is your color."

Carol held the shirt to her nose. In front of Sandra, she didn't feel embarrassed. She inhaled Jennifer's adult scent, rose and musk. Not the forsythia she'd worn in high school.

The closet emptied. After Sandra left, dragging the Housing Works bags, Carol sat in the closet and stared at the mattress. Strangers would be by later to take it away. Drew had posted an ad on Craigslist, but he hadn't written why they were selling, what had happened to Jennifer. Carol felt the omission unfair. The new owners might have Jennifer's dreams. They were a couple, a man and woman, grad students. They would take the mattress to Hamilton Heights in the van they'd rented, giddy about their fantastic deal.

Carol listened to the apartment. The slow hiss of steam in the pipes. The neighbor's parakeet, talking to itself. A squeak that could be a mouse, and footsteps, far away.

Good-bye, she thought, because it felt like what she was supposed to be thinking.

Good-bye, good-bye, good-bye.

She should have taken the whole wardrobe.

Jennifer's clothes: a charcoal pencil skirt with a shimmery purple tank top. Carol bought hose like ones she saw in Jennifer's dresser, black, with a seam up the back. She brushes out her hair until it falls in waves over her shoulders. The makeup takes the most time, although less than it used to. The result would make Jennifer proud.

Carol zips up her boots. As she turns her head, the cross earrings swing.

When the phone rings, she allows herself to imagine, just for an instant, that Jennifer might be on the other end, inviting her out for the night.

"Carol. It's Julie."

She fingers the earrings, the bump of the stones.

"Oh," Carol says. "Have you reconsidered the chairs?"

"Drew told me."

"He told you?"

"About Jennifer. Dear, I am so sorry."

"Yes," Carol says. "Thank you."

"Do you want me to come over?"

"Why?"

"To be with you. I thought you might need someone."

"No. But thank you."

"Carol, is Drew there?"

"I'm not sure. I don't think so."

"He said he was looking for Ben. I didn't know which Mike, but I reached all of them except the McMillians, and I think they're in Hawaii."

"Ben's okay."

"I'm sure he is—"

"Ben's okay." Carol shifts back and forth on her heels. "He's fifteen."

"It's almost eleven."

"Spring break."

"Carol, let me come over."

"Thank you for calling."

She puts the receiver back in the cradle.

She is not worried about Ben. He has never given her reason to worry, not ever before.

Jennifer's blue suede jacket lies heavily across her shoulders. Without the belt, it does not contour to Carol's shape as it did to Jennifer's, but that bothers her only vaguely. What matters is Jennifer's smell. Rose and sweat and forsythia, too, light, the memory of girlhood imprinted over the other memories made in this coat. Carol twists in front of the mirror, making sure the seams of her stockings line up. Her daughter's fingers tug at the hem of her skirt. She sees Jennifer's lips pucker and press as she applies a final coat of lipstick.

She tosses her cell phone toward the bed, leaving it behind as Jennifer left hers. It lands on the floor, where it will stay until she returns, or until Drew discovers it—she will pretend she didn't know.

Thirty-Seven

These are Jennifer's friends, and they pat him on the back, hand him a glass of wine, make room for him on the couch, and pass him the hookah. "Ben," they say. "Jen." They smile at the rhyme, and he likes it, too, wishes they had been Ben and Jen within the family, wishes his family had had this kind of warmth, bodies touching bodies with no requests, no obligations, just to be close. Now that he has it, he understands what Jennifer craved, what made her stay away.

Jen. Ben.

He holds the cherry-flavored smoke in his mouth and blows out in one smooth line. He doesn't cough, doesn't even worry about coughing. The girl next to him has braids in her hair and torn fishnet tights. She puckers and blows a shaky smoke ring. Someone claps. Sandra stays near. She sits on the arm of the couch, lays her torso along the back so that she is draped behind him and he can smell her Sandra smell, which seems like his smell now.

Trey ducks through the open window, out onto the fire escape, where people gather, their laughter drifting back inside. In the corner two men in suits who look like old mobsters hunch over an instrument, plucking at the strings, sending out throbs and moans that remind Ben of the music at the Indian restaurant the night before, only discordant. "Sitar," Sandra says into his ear before he has a chance to ask. "They have a cabaret act with her." She points to a short, round woman sitting cross-legged on the floor. "She sings like a dream."

The woman hears them and smiles. Ben has never seen such an orderly face; she looks like a doll. "We are *not* using that in the show," the woman says. "No hippie shit."

The sitar player wearing the Clark Kent glasses looks up. "We'll see," he says.

"Um, no, we won't."

"I like it," Sandra says. "You can play it at the exhibit opening. Add a little atmosphere. What do you think, Ben?"

"Okay," he says, but he doesn't think the sitar is right for Jennifer's pictures. Her photographs should be viewed in silence, reverence.

He looks into the faces of her friends, trying to fit each feature into Jennifer's life. Where did she sit? Whom did she know best, aside from Sandra? Whom did she love? Whom did she trust?

He wants all their stories. He wants to feel the shape of all her nights.

As he looks around the circle, he realizes that none of them came to the vigils. Only Sandra was there, cupping the candle between her palms, putting her arm around his mom, joining the dozens of others—neighbors, friends from high school, strangers—holding up flyers with Jennifer's photograph for the television cameras. Sandra didn't stay afterward. She slipped away without even saying good-bye.

When the hookah arrives again at his elbow, he passes it on. The wine is a deep red, almost purple, and tastes the way the color should.

The sitar screeches.

Ben's phone vibrates. The girl with the braids shifts slightly, and he takes out the phone, shuts off the vibrator, so as not to be rude. His dad again.

"Maybe you should answer that," Sandra says.

He shakes his head.

"Suit yourself."

He turns his phone off and disentangles himself from the sprawled bodies. "Bathroom?" he says, and the girl with the braids points through the kitchen.

The bathroom is dirty enough for Ben to notice. He pees and sits on the edge of the tub, staring at his sneakers. The wine has left a metallic taste in the back of his mouth. He turns his head and spits purple into the drain.

A knock at the door.

"Just a second."

"It's me," Sandra says.

The space is too small for both of their bodies. Pushed up so close, he is tempted to kiss her again.

He inclines his chin down, ready.

"Having a good time?" she says, looking around him into the mirror. She rearranges the petals in her hair.

"Yeah," Ben says. "It's all right."

"Pretty low-key. We'll move on soon. I just wanted to come by since it's Simon's birthday."

"Which one's Simon?"

"The bald dude."

He hasn't noticed anyone bald.

"Why didn't they come to her vigil?" he asks.

Petals fall into the sink. Ben has to stop himself from picking them up.

"Oh," Sandra says. "We did our own thing."

"When?"

"A while ago. When we knew she was really gone."

"You could have told me."

In the mirror, Sandra gives him a small smile. "It was just for us. You being there would have complicated things."

He doesn't see what would have been so complicated about it. "What was it like?" he asks.

"Beautiful. Thalia sang. We made a circle of candles and sent out energy to help her. To send her toward peace."

"What peace?"

Sandra stops messing with her hair.

"Not tonight," she says. "You wanted to come along, so you have to get in the spirit. It's Friday. We're having fun."

She spreads her hand across Ben's chest.

"Okay?" she says, pressing right into his heart. "Can you do that?"

"Okay," he says.

Trey steps through the window, followed by a bald guy who must be Simon.

"Happy birthday," Sandra shouts, springing up from the couch to hug him. He holds Sandra's wrist between his thumb and forefinger.

"Looking good," Simon says.

Sandra motions Ben over.

"Simon did our knots," she says. "When you're ready, we'll have Simon do yours."

"I'm ready now," Ben says.

"Uh-uh. Remember, we had a deal. Wait—"

"No." Ben doesn't like her tone, speaking to him as if he were a child in front of Jennifer's friends. She's different tonight. Running hot then cold. "I'm ready now," he says.

She darts to the desk in the corner and returns with a black Magic Marker. Taking Ben's wrist firmly in her hand, she says, "What do you want?"

He hesitates.

"You're ready," she says. "Now tell me what you want."

Simon and Trey stand on either side of Sandra, watching. Ben feels the focus of the party shifting behind him, away from the hookah and toward the action.

Sandra presses down with the marker.

"A knot?" she says.

"Her initial."

Sandra makes a swooping design that could be a *J*, could be an *S*. The chemical smell tickles Ben's nose. The ink burns.

"Hold your arm out," she says. "Let it dry."

"Not bad," Simon says.

Sandra caps the marker with a pop. "You like?"

Ben stares at his wrist. At least now there's something there.

Thirty-Eight

Drew lays his full weight on the buzzer, angry at himself. He should have stayed the course and not budged from that love seat until he had loosened his family from her grips. What had he been thinking? A bar. Searching for honesty by going to the least honorable of places. Stewing in self-pity. Of course Jennifer hated him. She saw through his posturing; she called him out on his hypocrisy, and he resolutely, obstinately refused to admit his faults.

A phony. Buzz. A sham. Buzz. A poor excuse for a father. Buzzzzzzzzzzzz.

He peers through the window. There is no light in the entryway; he can barely make out the corner of the stairs. Behind him the street ripples with life. At the restaurant at the end of the block a crowd swarms, their voices mingling with the music spilling out the open door. The night, just starting. Normally Drew would be in bed.

He drops onto the stoop, thinking about Carol, wishing she were here with him, so he wouldn't have to search for their son alone. He doesn't expect her to be home when he gets back. He imagines her pushing hangers around the closet, deciding which outfit to wear for whomever she has chosen to wait for her, to comfort her. She used to take forever to get ready, fretting in front of the mirror, changing outfits several times. The night they met she had been wearing a new black dress, bought specifically for the party. For years she kept it as a memento until one day, when he hadn't seen it for a while, he looked for it and discovered that it had been packed off to Housing Works "ages ago."

Unlike Jennifer, Carol has never realized her beauty, never had the confidence of a beautiful woman. Her timidity is part of what attracted him. He liked the way she stayed by that window, gazing out at Manhattan, as if the party raging behind her did not exist. He felt compelled to approach, to see if she would accept him; he wanted the challenge of entering her world. Her openness made him feel important. Powerful. She used to cling to him. Then they had Jennifer, and Carol clung to her.

It was destructive for a mother to worship her daughter. He worried that Jennifer would grow up spoiled, and she did, although she had his edge to prevent her from becoming soft. From infancy she fought anyone who dared restrain her. Carol caved, Drew fought back, and Jennifer became rebellious, her mother's greatest love. Her father's, too.

And Ben. Ben has always been more like Carol, waiting for someone to notice, to offer him something to cling to. The perfect disciple—the perfect prey—for a woman like Sandra.

"It's eleven thirty, bud. You're not in trouble, but you have to call me. You have to let me know you're all right."

He calls home. When the answering machine picks up, he tries Carol's cell.

"Please," he says. "Be careful."

When Ben was five, Drew lost him in Fairway. He never told anyone, not even Carol, and over the years he'd forgotten about the incident until now, sitting on Sandra's stoop, unable to find his son again. It was a Saturday morning, and Drew was fighting his way through the weekend crowd to the fish at the back of the store, confident that Ben was following behind. But when he turned around, his son wasn't there. Drew had never felt such panic—his heart sped up; his vision narrowed. Every face complicit, culpable, his mind careening to the worst although that worst paled in comparison to what he knows to be the worst now. The whole episode lasted less than ten minutes. Ben, good kid that he was, had gone to a checkout and told the lady at the register that he couldn't find his dad. Drew's name was announced over the loudspeaker, and when he ran to the front of the store, there Ben stood, holding a manager's hand, his expression serious but his tears dried.

Drew bought Ben an ice-cream cone, a bribe not to tell his mother. On the way home, he gripped Ben's hand and lectured him about staying close, not wandering off, although Drew knew that he had been the one to do the wandering. He had been the one who lost track. Ben licked his ice cream and nodded, saying nothing, but Drew understood that he was taking everything in—the throbbing traffic on Broadway, the men and women surging across the intersection, and most of all, Drew prattling on above him.

Drew stares at the building across the street from Sandra's so long that the bricks lose focus and begin to dance. He shifts on the step to bring blood back into his thighs. At the end of the block, the crowd thins, the music coming only in bursts now when the door opens, expelling one more well-fed, tipsy couple out into the rest of their night. He keeps his cell phone in hand, but an hour has passed with no response from Ben. Sandra, a nocturnal creature, will not be back until morning. He is wasting time here, but he doesn't know where else to go.

A woman carrying a paper Trader Joe's bag stops at the base of the stoop. She is older than Sandra, younger than Drew, her hair tucked up beneath a floppy knit cap, loosely woven. "Hello," she says lightly, but her eyes give him a quick up and down and seem to decide on the negative.

"Do you live here?" Drew asks.

The woman puts her booted foot on the first step, claiming her territory. "Yes," she says, "and you don't."

"I'm looking for Sandra."

"Ah." The woman proceeds past him. "Why not leave her a note?" She points to the doorframe. "Slip it inside."

"I think she's with my son."

The woman fishes keys out of her giant tote bag.

"He's fifteen," Drew says, rising.

She looks at him over her shoulder as she unlocks the door. "What's he look like?"

"About this tall." Drew holds his hand at his shoulder. "Light-brown hair. Looks young for his age. He's wearing a T-shirt. Black, I think."

The woman is nodding, the grocery bag balanced on her hip. "I did see them," she says, "with that boyfriend of hers."

That boyfriend. His son out there, somewhere, with the punk with the dragon tattoo.

"When?" he says.

"Early. Maybe eightish."

"Where did they go?"

"How should I know?" She flicks her fingers eastward. "Thatta way."

Drew looks off in that direction.

"Here." The woman hands him the grocery bag, which is heavier than he expects—he almost drops it—and digs around in her tote, producing a pen and a small notepad, the paper light blue, a sun-and-moon design in the corner.

Sandra, he writes, aware of the woman watching over his shoulder, *I'm looking for Ben. Please send him home.*

He adds his cell phone number and holds out the pen and paper. The woman nods toward her tote, and he drops them inside.

"Thank you," he says.

"Are you done lurking?"

"What?"

"Are you done?"

"I guess I am."

"Good luck," the woman says.

After she closes the door, she stays by the window and watches as Drew crouches and slips the note through the crack around the frame. Their eyes meet. She makes a shooing motion, and when Drew doesn't move, she mimes talking on the phone. He gets it: time to go.

Thirty-Nine

The bartender pretends not to remember her, but Carol notices her eyes lift in recognition. It's still early, and Carol has the place to herself except for two men in suits tucked into a corner, checking their cell phone screens. At the DJ booth, a woman with green dreadlocks curling from her head like serpents sips from a bottle of water and fiddles with a laptop.

"Kamikaze," Carol says. She assumes Jennifer chose the drink for its name more than its taste. Jennifer and Sandra, out on the town, two kamikazes.

She waves her fingers over the votive candle, dipping her nails in toward the wax, flicking the sides of the holder. Sandra took Jennifer's candles, packed them up in an old fruit box and arranged them across her coffee table in no discernable order. When Carol asked why Jennifer had them, Sandra said she liked the way they looked: lights out, candles scattered, like living among the stars. But such an answer is too simple. The saints had to mean something. Jennifer must have known, on some level, that she would need their guidance.

Carol never went to church, not even as a child. On Sundays she stayed home with her father and watched cartoons while her mother dressed—hat, white gloves, heels—and went to services at the Presbyterian church down the block. Carol treasured those mornings with her dad, the only time they spent hours together in the same room, even if the newspaper occupied more of his attention than she did. Sometimes they laughed at the cartoons at the same time.

"You pray enough for all of us," her father would say, and her mother would bat his arm with her gloves. Carol realized later that church had very little to do with spirituality for her mother. Sunday morning meant a chance to dress up, gossip with her friends, flirt with the attractive young preacher, be an adult without an irritable husband and sullen kid in tow.

Carol twists the crosses dangling from her ears. She can't explain what compelled her to take them except that they were right there, in the old cigar box Sandra uses for her jewelry, like an omen, talismans: the lid open, the earrings on top of a tangle of necklace chains, those blue stones. She heard the toilet flush, and the earrings went into her pocket. Later, when she put them on, she felt a brief surge of joy, her first since Jennifer vanished. They look so right, the blue stones against her dark hair. The crosses connect her to the candles, to the religion that never meant anything to her and still doesn't mean anything, except that she understands loss now, she understands annihilation of the body, humiliation of the soul, and she is reaching out, reaching up, to whatever might be out there, where Jennifer lives now.

Forty

They leave with Simon and the girl with braids. Simon loops his arm around the girl, although Ben isn't sure if they came as a couple or are just becoming one now. While Trey walks on ahead with them, Sandra threads her fingers through Ben's and swings their hands between them.

"Sorry I disfigured you," she says. "I was trying to prove a point."

"It doesn't look bad," Ben says, twisting his arm around to see the Magic Marker swoop.

"Fair warning, I can be a bitch sometimes."

"Is Trey your boyfriend?"

"Trey is Trey," she says.

Inferno looks like nothing from the outside, just a small warehouse or oversized garage, but a heavy beat pounds the sidewalk every time the bouncer opens the door. Ben can't believe they're here; he has imagined this place countless times. He wants to go inside and he doesn't, but the choice isn't his anymore. The night is happening, with him inside it.

Trey ignores the line. He doesn't even have to say anything; he just looks at the bouncer, and the door is opened and the five of them step through.

Sandra keeps hold of Ben's hand past the bar and around the tables, through the churning sea of sweating bodies. It takes him a moment to notice that she is rubbing her thumb against his. He is underdressed, feels like a nobody in a room full of somebodies. He bends down to say something to Sandra, seek reassurance, but she is focused straight ahead, where Trey is cutting them a path. Already Simon and the girl with braids have disappeared.

In the back, off to the right, there is a clear space where they can stand together. Sandra lets go of Ben's hand. Feeling sweat on his arm where it pressed against her, he looks down and checks his fake tattoo. It hasn't smeared. He's liking it better, the *J* or the *S*.

"Now?" Trey says.

Sandra nods, holds out her hand.

The bathroom is unisex; Ben has never seen anything like it. The floors and walls resemble stone, but the stalls look like the ones at school. An old man in a suit slumps on a folding chair beside the door, next to a wicker basket of paper towels, another of gum and suckers, a third of dollar bills and loose change. In front of the mirror, below red light bulbs, women, men dressed as women, and a few men dressed as men preen, getting beautiful only to sweat it all away.

Trey and Sandra and Ben cram into the end stall. From next to them come the unmistakable sounds of people having sex.

It takes some time for Trey to fish the plastic bag out of the pocket of his tight jeans.

"One," Sandra says, and Trey grimaces.

"And a half," he says.

"One."

Trey passes out one pill to each of them. On Ben's palm, it looks innocuous. Smaller than an aspirin.

Sandra opens her mouth, pops the pill inside. The stall wall vibrates with the weight of a body. Trey pounds back with his fist.

Ben has a hard time swallowing without water. The pill leaves a chalky, astringent aftertaste, but he tries to keep his face from showing it.

On their way out, he drops a dollar into the old man's tip basket. The man nods gravely, and Ben feels guilty, complicit in a great indignity.

Forty-One

Drew heads east because the woman in the floppy hat flicked her fingers east. It's as good a reason as any other, although he suspects the finger flick was arbitrary. By now Sandra and Ben could have moved on anywhere. With this thought, he turns south. At each intersection he lets his body choose, hoping to be guided by some sort of latent paternal instinct.

The Lower East Side is foreign to Drew. For his parents, this was the realm of immigrants, with all the associated violence, grit, and disease, a place to leave quickly and avoid once you'd gone. When Drew was growing up in Queens, artists, radicals, and junkies populated the Lower East Side, but he had no business with them, no interest in art or revolution; as a teenager, he bought his pot from a guy in Flushing. Later he came here with Carol on double dates with work colleagues to some hot new restaurant or another. He despised the artifice, stood on lines disbelieving anything could be innovative enough about this wine bar or that fusion bistro to warrant the half-hour wait, and was always proven right.

When Jennifer announced her intention to move here, he thought she was chasing the Lower East Side's ghost. Bohemian by association. Increasing her artistic prospects by breathing in the hallowed air. It seemed naïve, immature. She would be better off finishing her degree. But Carol embraced the idea. "I wish I'd had the courage to do something like that at her age," she said, and Drew pointed out that she'd moved from Ohio to New York on her own when she was only a little older, no small feat.

"But I didn't have her confidence," Carol said.

She went to check out the apartment Jennifer had so proudly found herself. The arrangement struck Drew as dubious—the woman who had rented the apartment for thirty years now lived in Florida; Jennifer would be her off-the-books sublessee, sending off a check each month for two hundred dollars more than the rent-controlled amount. These illegal sublets happened all the time in the city, and they enraged Drew. "That's why Manhattan market rate is so damn high," he said, and Carol said, "Please. It's not the only reason."

He should have been relieved, since they ended up covering most of Jennifer's rent. She did get a job at a coffee shop, making barely above minimum wage. "Plus tips," Carol said, but who tips at a coffee shop?

Carol didn't tell him about the money she gave Jennifer. She used cash, as if he wouldn't notice the increase in ATM withdrawals. But he tried not to complain. It would have been better if Jennifer had stayed in school, but at least she'd stayed in New York. Enough distance existed between the Lower East Side and the Upper West Side for all of them to breathe, but not enough for them to lose each other. Or so he had thought.

It amazes him how much he took for granted. How untouchable he used to feel. As if the worst thing that could happen was paying a high rent he could afford; as if his archnemesis was his own daughter, mirroring his surly stubbornness back to him across the dinner table.

He stops in front of her old apartment, surprised to see it, as though his thoughts conjured the building up. He touches the bricks. In daylight they have a yellowish cast, but there is no light in the vestibule, no lights on this pocket of Suffolk Street. The door is locked, although there is a brick pushed off to the side. When he first came with Carol, the door was propped open and Jennifer had been missing for two weeks. He hadn't been invited before; he had never invited himself. Their footsteps fell heavily on the metal stairs. The apartment was long and narrow, the kitchen off one end, the bedroom off another, just big enough for a double bed. She didn't have a frame, just a mattress on the floor.

"Did you know about this?" he said to Carol, but she was busy going through Jennifer's closet. He sat on the mattress. The police had asked them to come, to help evaluate if anything was amiss. But nothing in the apartment made sense to Drew, except Jennifer's photographs. Those he recognized. As Carol went through the clothes—why did she fixate on the clothes?—he went through the binders, the proofs, spread out across Jennifer's desk. Two big canvas prints were stacked against the wall next to the couch, an ugly thing smelling of mildew, which he would learn had been found on the curb and dragged up those metal stairs.

One canvas showed the back of a woman smoking on a fire escape. The other, a naked man in the shower. Drew looked once and turned the canvases away.

She had two cameras, a digital and a manual, thirty-five millimeter. He looked through both, aimed them around the room, trying to witness the world through her eyes.

He accidentally took a picture of his foot.

"Put that down," Carol said.

She stood in the doorway, her arms full of clothes.

"You might break it."

"It's just a camera," he said.

She flinched, but he hadn't meant it that way.

"I'm going to ask Sandra to come over," Carol said. "She'll know more than we do."

He put the camera back in its case, on the desk, where he had found it.

"Who's Sandra?" he said.

"It's after midnight." He tries to keep his voice from shaking. "Ben, if you don't call me back in the next half hour, I'm going to call the police."

His phone battery is getting low, but he doesn't dare shut it off.

Forty-Two

She dances, dances, dances.

She is Jennifer, she is all the girls in their beauty and their youth, she is herself at twenty-four, newly arrived in the city, braver than she's ever been, circling her hips, swinging her hair, opening her mouth wide and singing, singing words to songs she doesn't know, songs she realizes she's known forever.

Jennifer's jacket sticks, a second skin.

The DJ gives her a thumbs-up, and Carol lets loose, knees lifting, arms pumping, a scream building up in her throat.

This—*this*—is living.

This—just this—is enough to kill for.

Forty-Three

Ben's stomach cramps. He rushes back to the bathroom, where a line has formed. He tightens his muscles, worried that he will shit himself, and in a flash he hates the preeners, hates all the people slipping into stalls in twos and threes.

Sandra comes to check on him.

"Breathe," she says, rubbing his back. "Here." She presses a water bottle against his sweaty neck, and he concentrates on the stone floor, praying he won't pass out.

It's supposed to feel good, but he doesn't feel good.

"Sandra?"

"Yes, baby?"

Another spasm renders him speechless. He grips her hand.

When a stall finally opens, he bolts inside and slides the lock. He hangs his head between his knees and breathes as he was told. His body empties. The pain subsides.

Outside, Sandra has joined the preeners in front of the mirror. The last of the petals have fallen from her hair, onto the bathroom floor.

"All right?" she says.

He nods.

"That's never happened before?"

She's testing him, proving another point.

He washes his hands.

"Not usually," he says.

"You'll be fine." She touches his shoulder lightly with her fingertips. "Just stay by me."

That's been his plan all along.

Forty-Four

"911. What is your emergency?"

"My son is missing."

"Your son is missing?"

"Yes, that's correct."

"Sir, can I have your first and last name?"

"Andrew Bauer."

"How old is your son?"

"Fifteen."

"And his name?"

"Ben. Benjamin."

"All right, sir. When and where was he last seen?"

"This afternoon. At home. He told his mother he'd be back at seven, and now it's almost one."

"Sir—"

"It's almost one, and he's not answering his phone."

"Sir, Mr.—"

"Bauer."

"Mr. Bauer, is your son mentally or physically impaired?"

"No."

"He's fifteen?"

"Yes."

"Does he have a history of running away?"

"No, never. I think he's with a friend of my daughter's. Sandra. I don't know her last name."

"Sir, I'll connect you to your local precinct, and you can file a report, but I recommend waiting until morning. Teenagers—"

"I'm Jennifer Bauer's father."

"Sir?"

"Jennifer Bauer. She was abducted. Killed. She's dead. You guys are working the case. You're supposed to be working the case."

"I'm sorry, sir. I'm not familiar with—"

"Goddamn you, I'm not waiting until morning. Put me through."

Forty-Five

When she looks up, he is standing at the perimeter in his pin-striped suit, watching, exactly how she imagined him to be: the still point in the room.

"You're a good dancer," he says, and there's an accent she can't quite place.

"Join me."

"Not my kind of dancing."

They stand side by side. In these heels, she is almost his height—she could look him straight in the eye, but he is looking at the dancers. A sharp chin, wide cheekbones. Gray at the temples, premature.

Hazel eyes.

Once she has his eyes, she won't let go.

"I'd like a drink," she says, and he takes her by the elbow, steers her over to a table.

"What would you like?"

"Surprise me."

At the bar he waits patiently for an opening. The bartender pays him no special attention. She works automatically, efficiently, skilled at her job. After he makes his request, he swivels on his heels and lifts his hand, securing their connection. Carol does the same: raises her hand, holds it there.

Champagne.

"What are we celebrating?" she asks.

"Do we need a reason?"

The accent is British, but slight, his parents' accent or boarding school or an affectation.

"Aren't you hot?" He reaches across the table, pinches the jacket collar.

Carol drinks without answering.

His hazel eyes crinkle up at the corners. They are not the cool eyes of the serial killers on the computer screen, those glowering mug shots and crazed grins, those vacant stares and animal eyes. Of course not. She is seeing what Jennifer saw: a real man. A gentleman in an expensive suit and a crisp white shirt, the top two buttons undone. A gold wristwatch. Long, thin fingers, nails neatly trimmed.

"I'm Marcus."

His hand, smooth in hers.

She lets go quickly.

"Jennifer."

He doesn't even blink.

"Pleasure to meet you, Jennifer."

Forty-Six

Bubbles float up through his blood, tickling his bones. They make him a little nauseated, but his stomach has stopped quivering. He is more curious than scared.

In her tight blue dress, Sandra dances.

Within the chaos, he focuses on the sway of her hips. They remind him to move his own. They are dancing together. Trey is there, too, but when Ben turns his head to the left, he disappears. Trey doesn't matter anyway. What matters is Sandra in blue, her swaying hips, her hands kneading the air like a cat's. That afternoon, lazy in the sun, they were cats together. He stroked her hair, made her purr, so now he puts his hands up, mimics her gesture, two cats at play. Even though she has her eyes closed, he makes the sound in the back of his throat. Purr. Purrrrrr. It makes him laugh, and now she is laughing, too, eyes open, looking at him in delight.

She is happy, he is happy, and something amazing is about to happen. He can feel it in his bones.

Forty-Seven

The deeper he goes, the more disoriented he becomes, lost within this catacomb of streets. Although the police took down Ben's description, he knows they will do little, if anything. After a year, they have not found Jennifer's abductor; most likely they never will. If he is going to save what is left of his family, he has to take matters into his own hands.

And so he walks along the shadows, peering into their depths, aware of the history layered within, the millions of births and deaths stacked one on top of another, a warren of forgotten voices, forgotten faces, extinguished thoughts. Living, he is the trespasser. Whole blocks pass in darkness, with only a light or two in a window to indicate that anyone is still awake, still watching. On other blocks music rumbles, young people tumbling out of low-lit doorways, hailing cabs. He searches their faces—bright and open, closed and warning, all too familiar, none the ones he's searching for. As the night wears on, they vanish. The figures become solitary, pausing to light cigarettes, careening along the sidewalk, stumbling into the empty street. He steps around vomit. He steps around broken glass. He steps around a passed-out body stinking of booze and shit. He hears raised voices, emanating from nowhere.

In his pocket his cell phone remains silent, the last of its battery dwindling away.

He has no idea where Sandra would take Ben—in a city this large, this full of transgressions, the possibilities are infinite.

Remembering the way Sandra held his hand, the way he responded to her touch, with such desperation, such need—the way he had reached for her—he sinks down deeper into the darkness that has opened for him, unrecognizable to himself.

The futility of this walk is clear, but Drew can't stop; he must keep putting one foot in front of the other. The night becomes less of a search and more of a punishment. Penance for all those years of having his head stuck up his ass.

Forty-Eight

"I'm an artist. A photographer."

His teeth are perfect pearls. He wears a cologne that she has smelled before on the subway, a scent favored by men who get off downtown, sprayed on too strongly by the young and overeager.

"What do you photograph?" he asks.

"The city."

The two undone buttons reveal the ridge of his collarbone. An indentation where her fingers would fit.

"You must never run out of subjects."

"No—"

"Take off your jacket."

"What do you do?" she says, unzipping the jacket partway.

"I appreciate art."

"You're an artist?"

"No. I appreciate art."

She keeps his attention even though the club is full, the choices many.

"You're too attached to that jacket."

"You don't like it?"

"I'd like to see what's underneath."

She'll surrender this, as a means to an end. The moment the jacket leaves her shoulders, she shivers.

"Better," he says.

His hazel eyes rove across her body.

"I'll get cold," she says.

"Not tonight."

While he gets them another round, she resists the urge to put the jacket back on. Exposure is a sacrifice she must be prepared to make.

This past year, Carol has tempted fate. She's stopped eating. Without looking, she's stepped into traffic and kept going against shouts and car-horn blasts. In the bathtub, she's submerged herself, but her eyes always pop open as she rises, sputtering, to the surface.

Alive or dead. She can't decide which is the better option, but she can't stay this way forever—in limbo, sentenced to purgatory.

She has to choose a side.

Marcus listens with his chin inclined, his eyes fixed on her eyes, on her throat, on her breasts, which the purple top accentuates so well. His attentive face reminds her of a fox's. As she tells him about her photography, her Lower East Side apartment, her best friend, Sandra, he demonstrates only patience and the casual interest of a man marking time, his true motives beyond this conversation. When she asks where he's from, he says he moved to New Jersey from London when he was seven. Hoboken. His parents and sister have since moved back.

"You're on your own, then," she says.

"Yes, I suppose so. In terms of family."

He claims that his job would not interest her, that it barely interests him. She appreciates his evasiveness. She would be disappointed to find out that he is as commonplace as an adman or project manager or, worse yet, in the same industry as Drew.

She licks her lips, hoping Jennifer's voice will find its way out. The candlelight glints off his gold cuff links, and yes, she is pleased—he is a man who wears French cuffs. She imagines his shirts on dry cleaner's hangers, a neat white row smelling of detergent, the abhorrent cologne laundered away. She touches his cuff and wonders where Jennifer was when he took the laundry in. Where did she leave her mark?

"Were you frightened to see me?" she asks.

"Excuse me?"

"Were you frightened?"

He smiles. "I don't think I understand."

Of course not. Fear is foreign to him. Jennifer would want a man capable of seizing the moment. *Carpe diem. Carpe noctem.*

Carol slips her hands over his.

"Surprised, at least," she says.

His forehead creases, but his smile widens—that perfect string of pearls.

"Look." She taps her glass. "All gone."

Forty-Nine

Music loops, he can't tell if it's the same song or a different song, the beat goes on and on, the beat the sped-up rhythm of his heart, the music *is* the heart, the beat pumping blood into the beast, he doesn't know how he didn't see it before, their shadows flung high on the wall, one animal, a single mass of twitching, tender flesh so beautiful beneath the throbbing lights, strange bodies no longer strange, strange bodies becoming your body, their heat your heat, their sweat your sweat, and when you look up, they look back, and you see yourself, grinning so hard your cheeks hurt, all one, together, forever, why didn't you see it before? It's so beautiful, so beautiful you want to cry—it feels so good to cry.

And in the center Sandra dances in her tight blue dress, her arms above her head, kneading the air like a cat.

Fifty

Drew's feet ache, but he keeps walking, circling the Lower East Side, the darkness so much a part of his blurred consciousness that he thinks he will always live this way, stumbling half-blind through the city.

Beneath the weak glow of a safety light, he sits down in a doorway, knees drawn to his chest, back against concrete, and takes out the notebook.

> I said, "That's my daughter," but I was wrong, it wasn't you. It was a lie. That photograph could have been anyone. It could have been staged. I should have demanded to see you in the flesh. I should have fought harder.
>
> I'm sorry I didn't fight harder.
>
> You can't help me now, and I have no right to even ask for help. But your brother is out there, with that so-called friend of yours, and so is your mother. I don't know either of them. I understand them even less than I understood you. How is it possible to live all together under one roof and not have any idea who the other people are? How can we love complete strangers so completely?

But we do. I do. That's what family is, strangers bound together, and in the end, it's all we have.

It's all I want.

I swear, I'll listen to anything you tell me. It's too late now, I know, but I'm ready to listen. I'll believe everything you say.

Jennifer—Jen—my daughter, my heart, please grant me the special power of restoring lost things, so that I may find peace.

Fifty-One

His hands work into the flesh on either side of her waist.

Her tongue stud flashes.

He kisses her with her mouth open.

The softness of her lips, the hard flick of metal.

He feeds off her. Off her touch.

He is touching her, or she is touching him; he can't tell the difference—it doesn't matter. They are one and the same.

They are the tissue at the very center of the beating heart.

"I love you," he says.

She steps back, squints up into his face.

"I love you," he says, but she can't hear. She's watching his lips; he says it again, slowly.

"I. Love. You."

"You love everyone tonight," she shouts and loosens his fingers from her hips.

She backs up, dancing away from his grasping hands.

Fifty-Two

The bubbles in the champagne enter her bloodstream, invade her brain, where they pop, pop, pop.

The music swells. His hand beneath hers is as smooth as her children's when they were babies. Their knees touch, hard bone against hard bone, only a thin barrier of fabric between.

After the third round, she can wait no longer.

"What are we still doing here?" she says.

Her hip knocks into the table, overturning the candle, which has already gone out. He offers her his arm, and she leans against him, as Jennifer leaned. She rests her head on his shoulder.

———

Sandra has been lost, swallowed up by the crowd. Ben pushes his way through. His blood no longer bubbles; it moves slow and thick, his limbs clumsy, his body cumbersome, an object he would like to leave behind. He runs into the bar, jarring his hip, and uses it to prop himself up. The front of the club has emptied out, only a few couples lingering at the tables. He has no idea what time it is, hasn't thought about time for ages. From inside the club, there is no way to tell if it is night or day. He feels as if weeks have passed.

A woman stands up from the table in the far corner. As she wobbles on her heels, her date hurries to steady her and one of the red spotlights catches her shirt, a shimmery purple. Ben stares, confused. She looks like his mom, but not like her. A cross between his mom and his sister. Ben shuts his eyes—that can't be right. When he looks again, the man is opening the club door. The woman turns, smiles, before stepping outside, and Ben knows that smile. He misses that smile.

Before he can think of what to do, the door shuts and they are gone.

———

Drew's phone is dead. Next to the Williamsburg Bridge, he fishes change out of his pocket, regretting giving the woman in the gold top his quarters. Those stupid jukebox songs, easy-listening music for the old and wasted.

The pay phone is scarred with graffiti, the change return stuffed with wads of Kleenex and Drew doesn't want to know what else. But miraculously, the phone works.

He calls Ben; he calls home. He listens to his son's voice, his wife's voice, telling him to leave a message. He hangs up and watches a man push a shopping cart filled with trash bags from one side of the underpass to the other. When he sees Drew watching, he raises a hand. Drew returns the gesture.

Inferno, he remembers, is somewhere around here. It would be perverse for Sandra and Trey to take Ben there, but Drew doesn't know what sort of people they are, what they are capable of doing.

He picks up the phone again and calls information.

———

At the curb, Marcus raises his hand for a cab. Carol steps back.

"Wrong way," she says.

"My place."

She pushes off his arm.

"I thought—"

"It's not in this direction," she says.

He laughs, reaches for her.

"Too many bubbles," he says, catching her around the waist.

———

In front of Inferno, a small group huddles on the sidewalk. They wear next to nothing, just strips of black, leather, vinyl, outlandish shoes. The women hug themselves, bouncing on the balls of their feet to ward off the chill. They grab roughly at each other or sit on the curb, staring off into space, talking low, coming down. Their eyes pass over Drew.

"Got a light?"

The boy's eyes are outlined in black, blue teardrops painted in the corners. He has his arms around a girl with braids. She has her eyes closed, her body heavy, as if sleeping standing up.

Drew pats his pockets, even though he knows he doesn't have a light.

"Sorry," he says.

A taxi pulls away from the curb, another wedging in behind it.

The bouncer's girth is squeezed into a tailored suit, a wire dangling from his ear like a Secret Service agent. Giving Drew the once-over, he shakes his head, but he opens the door, the hour late enough even for the rejects.

———

Inside the cab, she shuts her eyes, telling herself they are just taking a different route, a shortcut. She feels his presence beside her, but once again she waits. Why is he being so timid? She grabs fabric, his pant leg or suit jacket sleeve. He responds by placing his hand on her thigh, slipping his fingers beneath the hem of her skirt. He kisses her, and his mouth tastes of nothing but champagne. She turns away, her forehead to the glass.

Through half-open eyes, she watches Manhattan slide by. The stores are gated, the windows dark. Only occasional neon indicates that this is the city that never sleeps. The witching hour. Jennifer's favorite time of day, even as a child. Carol cannot count the number of times she fell asleep while trying to put Jennifer to bed and woke up in the middle of the night on the floor, Jennifer reading a book or playing with dolls beside her, wide awake and perfectly content.

The cab stops. The air smells of fish.

With his arm around her, Marcus ushers her through a red door into a vestibule with yellow, flaking walls. "I'd recommend taking off those shoes," he says.

She follows him up the stairs, her boots slung over one shoulder, Jennifer's jacket over the other. They climb and climb. Her hose stick to the steps, grit getting inside, onto the soles of her feet.

She slows. He disappears above, and she stops, listens to his feet rattling up and up.

"Jen-ni-fer," he calls, each syllable echoing through the stairwell.

"Coming." She grips the banister, pulls up. Her boots drop and bounce down the stairs. As she hurries to retrieve them, her hose snag on the edge of a step and the hole expands, her toes exposed.

There's nothing she can do about that now.

When she reaches the top, she finds the door open. Marcus lifts the jacket from her shoulder, takes her hand.

"Jennifer, my dear, make yourself at home."

Fifty-Three

Ben heads back into the fray of bodies, searching for Sandra. Near the bathroom, he finds an empty corner and slides down the wall until he sits on the concrete floor. His jaw feels bruised, as if he's been punched. He massages the joint with his fingers, works his jaw up and down. He's thirstier than he's ever been in his life, but he can't manage the walk back to the bar. The bottle of water he was holding earlier is long gone, although he can't remember drinking it.

Coming out of the bathroom, a woman trips over him, catching the wall just in time. "Jackass," she says, and he pulls in his feet. He hugs his knees to his chest, tucks in his chin, makes his body as small as possible. The ground heaves, the music coming at him from all angles, demanding attention.

His brain is working slowly; it doesn't feel familiar. His mom was here, with a man. He thinks his mom was here. He kissed Sandra; that he knows. He said he loved her, and in some way, she said it back.

When he looks up, there are feet and legs, stilettos and boots, skin and skin and more skin. He looks higher, and there is Jennifer, in the middle of the mass, her blond hair whipping around her face, her fist raised, punching the air. She looks like she's having the time of her life.

His eyes are playing tricks on him. He blinks, and she's still there. And then she's gone, swallowed up as if she never existed. He misses her even though he knows it wasn't Jennifer, just another girl with blond hair.

"Here, kid."

Trey is next to him, knocking a bottle of water against his arm. Ben unscrews the cap but can't bring himself to drink.

"Tired?" Trey says, and Ben shakes his head.

Trey looks at him steadily.

"You're coming down," he says. "I'd give you another, but Sandra would kill me."

"I can handle it."

"Sorry, kid. You don't get to decide. Them's the rules."

"Is Sandra your girlfriend?"

"Are you going to drink that or what?"

Trey takes the bottle back. Water drizzles down his chin, wasted. He wipes his mouth with the back of his hand.

"Sandra isn't *my* anything," he says. "We don't believe in ownership. She's her own person, and so am I."

"Was it that way with my sister, too?"

"Let's not talk about your sister."

Ben is filled with sudden rage. He grabs the bottle; water arcs up, splattering the floor.

"Why not? What do you have against her?"

"Nothing." Trey holds up his hands. "Jesus, nothing. But tonight— I'm not in the mood, kid. Anyway, I've got nothing to tell you. You knew her better than me, right? You lived under the same roof for what, eighteen years?"

"Twelve," Ben says. "I was twelve when she moved out."

"All right, twelve years. I knew her for, like, one year. Two. And not, like, well."

"That's not what Sandra said. She said you and Jennifer—you and Jen—you two were close."

"She got it wrong, kid."

"Stop calling me that."

Trey looks away, toward the dancing.

"I saw you kissing her," he says.

Ben straightens his spine against the wall. "So?" he says, with as much confidence as he can muster. "She can do what she wants."

"Hey, I'm not faulting you, just saying I saw. She's one sexy woman. But I don't get her side. You're a little young for her, don't you think?"

"Age doesn't matter."

"Gotta be guilt," Trey says. "She feels sorry for you."

Ben crunches the water bottle.

"Shut up."

"And all that end-of-the-world shit. Who do you think you are, kid? You've been seriously scarred, haven't you? Damaged. It's sad, man. I feel sorry for you, losing your sister, your family going crazy and all, I really do, but it's sad."

Ben swings. Trey catches his fist, pushes it to the floor.

"Sandra won't like it if we fight," he says, his breath hot against Ben's face. He sits back, keeping Ben's hand pinned.

"You don't know anything about me," Ben says.

His elbow throbs. He tries to lift his hand, but Trey is too strong.

"Only that you've got a thing for older women," Trey says. "But I do know Sandra. Better than you. And I'm just telling you to be careful. Back off, or you're going to get hurt."

"Maybe you're the one who doesn't know her."

"Yeah?" Even in the dim light, Ben can tell that Trey's pupils are huge. They change his ordinary, ugly face into something demonic. "Did she tell you she was supposed to go with Jen that night?"

"She had the flu."

"Uh-uh." Trey shakes his head slowly. "She was healthy as an ox."

"So what? It doesn't make a difference."

"I was with her," Trey says.

He presses down hard, crushing Ben's fingers.

"I don't care," Ben says.

"Yeah? So what's this all about then? Your whole fucking family—"

"Leave my family out of this."

"Why was your dad over today?"

"What?"

"Yeah, your dad. You didn't know about that? I had to get out because he wanted to have some sort of secret meeting."

Trey smiles, eases up on Ben's hand.

"What was he doing there?"

"Don't know," Trey says, widening his eyes. "Guess he was after something."

———

After a night of looking, she is delivered to him too easily, leaning against the bar in a bright-blue dress, her body more curvaceous than Drew had imagined. She is talking to the bartender, a curly-haired woman in a tight tank top. They are laughing, their joy too much.

Drew grabs Sandra by the shoulder, spins her around to face him.

"Where is my son?" he says.

The remnants of a smile stay on her face. "What?"

"My son." He gives her a push, hitting her back against the bar. "Ben. Where is he?"

"Hey." The bartender takes hold of Drew's elbow. Her hand is firm, her arm tense. "Cut it out."

"This—" What? *Cunt. Bitch. Demon. Vixen.* None of the words are right, none enough. "She took my son."

"Took?" Sandra rolls her eyes at the bartender. "Please."

"Sir?" The bouncer appears, moving in front of Drew, trying to block Sandra, but Drew is not in the wrong here; he will not be shaken off.

"What happened to Jennifer?" he says.

"Your guess is as good as mine." Sandra twists, her shoulder slipping free. The bouncer angles his body so that Sandra disappears. Drew leans to the right, the left, but the bouncer keeps pace, surprisingly agile for someone so large.

The bartender glares at Drew. "Get out of here," she says.

"You heard the lady." The bouncer puts out his arms, as if he's about to hug Drew, and starts walking, forcing Drew backward, toward the door.

"You're liable," Drew says, "for what happens in your club."

"All right, sir. Keep moving."

"You don't know who that woman is. Or maybe you do." Drew stops, plants his palm in the middle of the bouncer's chest, shoves. The bouncer doesn't move an inch. Drew's never been in a physical fight before, and the possibility excites him. He would lose, terribly, but he is hungry for bloodshed, ready for revenge.

The bouncer says something into his earpiece, and suddenly there is another man, only slightly smaller, in a matching suit beside him. The space between the men and Drew narrows until Drew's back is to the door, the door is opening, they're stepping outside.

Drew stumbles onto the sidewalk. The men stand together, arms folded, sentinels at the gates of hell. Impassable.

"You're harboring a criminal," Drew says.

The men look at each other.

"That's no criminal," the big one says. "The only criminal I see is you if you don't get a move on."

"Where were you when he took Jennifer? Where was all this security then?"

The men say nothing.

Drew paces to the edge of the sidewalk. The ragtag group from earlier is gone, having left spent cigarettes in their wake. He crushes one under his foot, kicks the debris into the gutter. Sandra will not come out as long as he's here; they won't let her. But he is not about to leave his boy behind.

He walks to the end of the block and waits.

The sky is still dark, but the air is clear, morning creeping up.

———

Panting, Sandra appears before them, hair plastered across her forehead. "There you are," she says, her eyes darting toward Ben and away, as if she knows what they've been talking about. As if she's been caught in a lie.

"Kid's had enough," Trey says.

"I'm fine." Ben pulls his hand out from under Trey's. His wrist hurts, but he will not shake it out.

"There's shots up front," Sandra says, "if you're up for it."

Trey grins. "Breakfast food."

"Ben?"

"Yeah," Ben says. "Sure."

They turn and start toward the front before Ben has a chance to get up. His feet slip out from under him, and he lands hard on his butt. He tries again, using his hand along the wall for support.

He passes couples in tight embraces, solitary figures jumping up and down in the center of the dance floor, bodies slumped or pressed against the walls. Where earlier there was unifying triumph, now the club feels saturated in defeat. He notices the empty water bottles and gum wrappers littering the floor, skids on spilled ice. The stench of other people's sweat mixes with the pungency of wet leather, something like burnt plastic, a faint odor of vomit.

Why would his dad visit Sandra? Why wouldn't she tell him?

Healthy as an ox. The expression is *healthy as a horse*. Trey has reasons to lie, but even as Ben thinks it, he knows Trey is telling the truth. Ben isn't a real threat, to Trey or anyone.

Three shot glasses are lined up at the end of the bar. The bartender looks at Ben and cocks an eyebrow at Sandra.

"Don't ask," the bartender says, "don't tell."

Sandra and Trey pick up their glasses, clink them together, and down the shot before Ben has a chance to pick up his. The alcohol makes his nose tickle. It burns his throat on the way down; he slams the glass onto the bar, shakes his head, mouth clenched. Laughing, Trey slaps him on the back. He slings an arm around Ben's shoulders, pulls him close, as if they're buddies.

"For your suffering," the bartender says to Sandra, pouring another round. "Who was that asshole, anyway?"

"What asshole?" Trey says.

"No one." Sandra presses the glass to her lips, as if considering, then opens her mouth, downs the shot. She doesn't even wince. "Some crazy guy."

"He was bothering you?" Trey looks around. "He still here?"

"They took care of him."

Ben drinks. He wants to lie down, he wants to sleep, but instead he drinks, each shot going down easier than the last. Trey and Sandra lean into each other, closing Ben out. Trey runs his hand through her hair. He grips the back of her neck. She angles her face up.

They are kissing.

"You weren't sick," Ben says.

They don't move away from each other. He taps Sandra on the back, and she turns, licking her lips.

"Why didn't you go?" he says. "You weren't sick."

"What?"

"That night with Jennifer. Why didn't you go?"

Sandra glances at Trey.

"I *was* sick," she says. "I was throwing up."

"You were healthy as an ox."

"So what?" Her eyes flash. "I didn't want to go, okay? I didn't feel like it."

"And you did what? Watched TV?"

"I slept. I went to bed early, and I slept through until morning."

"Yeah, right."

"You don't have to believe me," she says. "That's your choice."

Trey smirks at Ben. He grabs hold of Sandra's hip; she wraps her arm around his waist, her fingers inching up beneath his shirt. They will go home together, Ben realizes. They will have sex, sleep underneath the quilt Sandra's mother made. They will be glad to be rid of him.

"Why was my dad over?" Ben says. "What did he want?"

Sandra throws back her head. "Fuck your dad," she shouts at the ceiling.

"Say it, sister," Trey says.

She punches Trey on the shoulder. "Shut up. God, you two!" But she keeps her arm around his waist, her fingers pressed against his sweaty skin.

"None of that has anything to do with me, okay?" she says. "I'm not responsible for what happened. I'm not your family's fucking grief counselor. I don't owe any of you anything. Not a fucking thing."

Over her head, Trey grins at Ben.

"You heard her," Trey says.

"Do your parents even own a gallery?" Ben says.

"What the hell kind of question is that? Go home, kid. The party's over."

"When's the exhibit? Give me a date."

Sandra shuts her eyes. It takes a moment for Ben to realize she is crying. "I wanted to help you," she says, "but you want too much from me."

"Sandra," he says, "have you been to the gallery?"

She doesn't answer.

"Sandra—"

"Yes, Ben," she says. "I have been to the gallery."

He wants to believe her, but he doesn't know how anymore.

———

Drew watches the door, thinking about the surveillance video, the last recorded seconds of Jennifer in this world. He should have been there that night, ready to grab her. To lift her up over the cracks in the pavement so that she would not slip through.

Every time the door opens, his body tenses, ready to spring to action. They trickle out slowly, the last of the late-night denizens.

And then there he is, in his cargo shorts and black T-shirt, sandy hair sticking up at odd angles as if he has just rolled out of bed. Hands jammed into his pockets. Shoulders pulled up around his ears. Alone.

Drew runs. He grabs hold of his boy, hugs him hard. He presses his face into his son's hair, inhaling the way he did when Ben and Jennifer were toddlers, breathing in this perfect child, his vibrant flesh and blood.

The bouncer says something. Drew holds up his hand. *Don't even try.* He looks over his son's head, at the lights spanning across the Williamsburg Bridge, and tightens his hold.

"Dad?" Ben is saying. "Dad?"

Drew turns them away from Inferno.

"I'm here," he says. "I'm right here."

Fifty-Four

Inside his domain, Carol allows him to woo her. She accepts his offer of water, sits down on the faux leather couch, digs her toes into the white shag rug. He has gone for a retro look, modish: geometric patterns, all black and white. Not bad taste but overly styled, trying too hard.

The mounted TV reflects their images: her straight backed, him moving around the kitchen alcove, coming forward with a box of Triscuits, a wheel of Laughing Cow cheese. He sets everything up on the coffee table—white, oblong—and starts spreading.

"You have a nice place," she says and means it. Too much effort is better than none. He keeps things neat. The bookshelf in the corner alternates rows of books—mostly hardcover, she can't read the spines from here—with art: a smooth sculpture of a woman dancing, back bent into a crescent; a record propped on an easel; a blown-glass vase, a black-and-white vortex.

He offers her a cracker loaded with cheese. She puts up her palm in response.

"I like it," he says, popping the cracker into his mouth. "A bit small."

"That's Manhattan."

"Yeah, but someday I'm going to buy a house and make it over to my specifications. Not in the city, of course. I'm not a millionaire. Maybe I'll go back to Jersey."

She doesn't want to hear about his dreams for the future.

"You're not hungry?"

She shakes her head. A stray speck of cheese dots his lip, and she thinks of Ben, always a messy eater. She has to clench her hands around her water glass to keep from reaching over, wiping his mouth.

He puts away the food and puts on music. She doesn't recognize the singer. A low female voice. A melancholy melody meant to be sexy.

On the couch, their thighs and shoulders touch. He discarded the suit jacket when they came in, and now he takes off the cuff links, drops each one on the coffee table. Clink, clink. Rolls up his sleeves. Dark hairs cover his arms. Up close, she notices that his face is grainy, stubble beginning to show.

"Care to dance?" he says and presents his hand.

"I thought you didn't dance."

"Not that kind of dancing."

She lets herself be swept up, his hand on her waist. He moves with ease, but the steps are rudimentary. They make a box with their bodies, over and over.

She tries to fall in love, the way Jennifer must have, looking into those fox eyes, but the cheese on his lip distracts her. She kisses him to make it go away.

They stop dancing. He holds her. Her lips stiffen, but he doesn't seem to notice. He bends her backward, like the sculpture on his bookcase. Her lower back twinges, and she pushes on his shoulders until she is upright.

"All right?" he says, and she nods.

He unbuttons his shirt slowly, giving her a show.

She won't undress for him. From this point on, she will comply, but she will not instigate. These are the rules she has set for herself.

It doesn't take long for him to lift off her shirt. He fumbles with her bra, and she stands there, annoyed, until finally the clasp gives, the bra falls from her shoulders. His warm skin presses against hers, his chemical cologne smell overtaking the rose. She touches his back and feels the jut of shoulder blades. He is skinnier than she imagined he would be. Their bones fit together. A pair of skeletons, clutching, and she thinks about Jennifer's supple, living flesh.

Without letting go, he walks her backward into the bedroom, his eager lips finding her eyebrows, her cheeks, her mouth, her chin. She is reminded of the golden retriever her uncle had, the way it would jump up on you, slobbering across your face. She falls onto the bed and, as he unbuttons his pants, turns her head away to take in the room. The walls are bare; the closet door open; the bed to the side, under the window, unmade. She lifts her hips over a tangle of sheets. To the left, on a card table: a desk lamp; a box of Kleenex Ultra Soft with a sunflower motif; a beaten-up copy of *The Stranger*; a photograph of a man, woman, teenage boy, and little girl posed on the summit of a mountain, hazy ridges beyond. They all wear canvas sun hats.

She turns the photograph over.

His pants drop to the floor. He crawls on top of her, and there is the expression she has been waiting for: his pearl teeth bared, his hazel eyes focused, his fox face shining with the hunt.

As he tugs at her skirt, saliva drips from his mouth onto her chest.

"Can you help me with this?" he says.

She sits up, unzips her skirt, and lies back down.

Once she is naked, he pauses, kneeling. His hands hover above her, tracing her curves in the air.

He doesn't seem to notice that her arms stay at her sides, that her lips meet his only when he puts his against them. The foreplay lasts less than a minute, and he is up again, into the bathroom, returning with a condom.

In the other room, the woman stops singing.

She feels pain when he enters her, and she is grateful for it. She concentrates on the pain to avoid any residual pleasure.

His hazel eyes squeeze shut.

She lifts her hands and wraps them around his throat, her thumbs meeting in the indentation of his collarbone.

He squeaks and grabs her wrists, forces her hands down, above her head.

"Sorry, babe," he says. "Not into that."

But he lets her go.

He grimaces, getting close.

She reaches up again.

He has his hands on top of hers, pulling her fingers back from his throat, when he comes.

Her wrists bend under his weight. He laughs as he maneuvers his body behind hers, twisting their legs together, kissing the nape of her neck.

"That," he says, "was something else."

His hands lie on top of hers, folded against her chest.

"You're a little crazy," he says.

She stares at the box of Kleenex, those yellow flowers against a bright-blue sky. After a while, Marcus reaches over and grabs a handful of tissues. The bed shifts as he cleans himself off.

"You want some water?"

"No," she says.

He gets up, tosses the tissues in the trash, turns off the light in the other room. As he gets back into bed, he is whistling.

"Do you like eggs?" he says.

"Eggs?"

"Pancakes?"

"Not especially."

"I make a mean French toast."

She holds herself still, willing him to shut up.

"Don't tell me to call you a cab," he says.

"I won't."

He kisses her shoulder and yawns loudly.

"In the morning," he says, "you'll have to give me your number."

Within minutes, he begins to snore.

Carol picks up the photograph. The man and woman look like nice people. The little girl has a gap-toothed grin, like Jennifer had one summer. The teenage boy reminds her of Ben.

Fifty-Five

They walk without speaking. Ben tries to keep his footsteps steady so his dad won't be able to tell how much he's had to drink, about the MDMA. He wants some of that joy back, but all he feels is the hollowness taking over. He wants to crawl off somewhere, into himself, where he can hide for a while and be left alone.

But his dad is here. His dad found him—Ben has no idea how. He doesn't seem angry, just sad. Ben looks at him sidelong, afraid to make eye contact, worried even more about what he would see in his dad's face than what his dad would see in his.

———

They should get in a cab, go home, but Drew can tell Ben isn't ready yet. He isn't ready either. They need to walk off the night; he needs time to think, to decide what to tell Ben about Jennifer, how.

Up ahead, lights interrupt the darkness. Drew can't believe it: the Cuban diner, open twenty-four hours and beckoning, welcoming them in.

"Hungry?" Drew says.

Ben looks up.

"Okay," he says, pushing open the door.

He slides into a booth while Drew goes up to the counter and orders rice and beans. In the silence, Drew's voice sounds strange, unwarranted in this place. He doesn't know the rituals. The man behind the counter is small with a gnarled face, gnomelike in his white uniform. He assembles the plate and takes Drew's money without saying a word.

Drew sits across from Ben, sliding the plate between them. He hands Ben a plastic fork, and they begin to eat. The rice is dry, the beans overcooked. Drew mixes them together and adds salt. He eats slowly, wanting to absorb the taste, wanting to enjoy the rice and beans as much as Jennifer enjoyed them.

"This is good," he says, even though it's not. Ben nods without looking up.

Only one other booth is occupied, at the back. As he eats, Drew stares at the man's broad shoulders, the decal of a bald eagle on his worn leather jacket, his straggly graying ponytail. This place has the aura of Jennifer's photographs: New York on its most human scale. If Drew had her camera, he would take a picture of the gnome leaning against the counter with his arms folded and eyes closed, white apron stained with beans and chili sauce. He'd photograph the stranger's broad back, that proud, defiant eagle. He'd snap a picture of the food before him, the colors distorted by the flickering fluorescent lights.

He would take a picture of his son. Ben's eyes are heavy, his cheeks flushed. He hunches over the food, playing with it more than eating. Normally Drew would tell him to sit up straight, stop messing around. But that's not the father Drew is anymore. Not tonight, anyway.

———

Ben feels his dad watching him. When his dad pointed out this place, Ben almost said he'd been here before, but caught himself. He doesn't know what is happening, how much he can let on.

He thinks about his mom, the secrets she's carrying. What was she doing at Inferno, in Jennifer's clothes? Who was that man? He hopes she isn't in love. Love hurts.

Ben tries to swallow and can't. The rice and beans lodge in his throat. He pretends to wipe his mouth and spits into a napkin.

His dad is staring past him with a strange expression—wonder, almost. Awe.

Ben turns to see what's there.

———

The man in the eagle jacket is leaving, revealing his companion.

Cleopatra.

She is exquisite.

Drew holds his breath, fearful that the slightest disturbance will make this mythological creature disappear. Her long black hair has a blue sheen, falling straight down her back, behind her shoulders, which are bare, revealed by her cream-colored gown. Her dark skin seems to radiate an inner light. She has her head lowered, but she is not eating. The table is littered with debris: Styrofoam cups, napkins, empty plates. As he opens the door, the man in the eagle jacket looks back at her, and in his face Drew reads disgust. They have had an argument. The man looks old enough to be her father; he is ugly, sinewy. Undeserving. Drew is thankful when he's gone.

She raises her head, looks at him. She smiles.

She seems to recognize Drew. There is warmth in her eyes.

"I'll be right back," he says to Ben. "Sit tight."

He stands next to her table.

"Hello," he says.

"Hello." She offers her hand, which is as large as his but slender, the nails French tipped.

"Please," she says. "Have a seat."

"You're someone very special," Drew says.

Her head dips demurely on her swan neck, as if she is used to hearing such things.

"My daughter knew you."

"Your daughter?"

"Jennifer."

Cleopatra sips from a Styrofoam cup. Orange soda. "Sweet pea," she says, "you're going to have to do better than that."

"She used to come here with a friend. You made her jealous."

Cleopatra laughs, a deeper sound than her voice.

"I make a lot of girls jealous," she says.

"I think you represented something to Jennifer."

"And what might that be?"

"I'm not sure. But you were important. And I'm glad I've gotten a chance to meet you."

"Where is Jennifer?"

"She's dead," Drew says.

Cleopatra sits back, a hand over her heart.

"Good lord, sweet pea. I am *so* sorry."

"I just wanted to say hello."

Drew plans to leave now, but he can't move. He can't stop looking at Cleopatra, trying to see her through Jennifer's eyes.

"What's your name, sweet pea?"

"Drew."

"I'm Daphne."

Her arm extends, rolling from the shoulder, to take his hand and hold it. He tries to shake the name from his mind. Not Daphne. Not whatever name she was born with.

"My daughter called you Cleopatra."

"Did she? Isn't that the best."

"She was a talented photographer. A really—a promising young woman."

"Tragic," Cleopatra says.

Her eyes look deep into his, pinning him down, uncovering a yearning he didn't know was there.

"Is there something else I can do for you, Drew? Sweet pea?"

He thinks of his wife, prone across another man's bed.

"I—"

"What is it?"

His throat constricts.

"Sweet pea?"

He pulls away. Cleopatra's hand clings, her nails digging into his knuckles. She frowns. "Now, sweet pea," she says. "At least take my card."

She opens a cream-colored clutch, takes out a crisp white business card, lays it on the table among the jumble of wadded-up napkins and stained plastic forks, the splatters of beans and spilled orange soda.

"Dad." Ben is standing beside him, pulling on his arm.

"Call after seven," Cleopatra says.

"Dad."

Drew backs up from the table. He looks down at his son, wondering how much he's heard.

———

Outside, on the sidewalk, his dad sobs. He tries to compose himself but only ends up making it worse, his features bulging, hideous. Ben has never seen his dad cry before; he doesn't know what to do, who that woman in the diner was, why she made this happen. He rubs his dad's back, but that makes him cry harder.

His dad is saying something about Jennifer.

"What?" Ben says, and then he hears the word: *dead*.

Jennifer is dead.

"I know," Ben says.

His dad looks up. "How?"

"I don't know."

But that's a lie.

"The world changed," Ben says, "when she left it."

His dad stares at him and slowly starts to nod. He puts a hand on Ben's shoulder, uses it to push himself straight.

"Let's go home, bud," his dad says.

Fifty-Six

Jennifer would call first.

"Elvis left the building?" she'd say, and Ben would give her the all clear.

She always brought something new: music on her iPod, food—a candy bar from England, a sticky pastry from Turkey, a bag of Indian spices. "Inhale it," she'd say, waving the bag of red or brown or yellow beneath his nose. It was as if she were coming home from traveling the world, not taking the C train uptown.

The last time he saw her, she said she was tired and they lay down on his bed, heads touching, and stared at the faded marks of glue on the ceiling, traces from the glow-in-the-dark stars their mom had put up when he was a baby and Jennifer had helped him take down when he turned ten. They were listening to a band Jennifer had gone to hear at Mercury Lounge the Saturday before. The music was good; Ben really liked it.

She would ask him the big questions.

"What's the meaning of life?"

"What happens after we die?"

"Do you believe in God?"

"Are people basically good or basically evil?"

He tried to give his answers honestly. She listened, asked questions, played devil's advocate, saved her own opinion for last. What they had been raised to believe by their parents didn't factor in, except as a starting point. Jennifer pushed him to think for himself.

The last time, she asked, "What will you do when the world ends?"

"That's just paranoid."

"No, I'm talking about real threats. War. Climate change. Natural disasters."

"Like Sandy?"

"Yeah, like Sandy, but much more extreme." She rolled to her side, facing him. "The earth is constantly evolving," she said. "Think about the dinosaurs. Life as we know it *will* end. Maybe not for us, but for our children, or their children."

Ben thought about it. "Can we do anything? I mean, if the world's going to end, it'll end."

"I think it'll be more gradual," Jennifer said. "A shift. Stages. We'll have time to adjust, if we're ready. And then we'll have to adjust again. And again. And slowly we'll be living in a totally different way. Like we'll have to see that man isn't king of the castle anymore."

"So what would I do to readjust?"

"Yeah, okay."

"I guess I'd try to prepare as best as I could. So I could adjust. I guess that's all any of us could do. Because we really don't know what's going to happen or when, right? We just have to prepare and be ready all the time."

"You're very practical," Jennifer said. "You'll be fine. Humans are resilient anyway. I mean, look at everything we've lived through. The Holocaust. Katrina. 9/11. Genocide in Africa."

"Not everyone lived."

"You know what I mean."

"What would you do?"

"Probably nothing."

"Like when Sandy hit."

Jennifer laughed. "I was sitting in the dark, taking pictures out the window, drinking my weight in merlot."

"So when disaster comes—"

"I'll be blissfully unprepared."

"You'll come to me," Ben said.

"Yep." Jennifer grinned at him. "That's why we make a good team."

Ben turns over this conversation as he rides beside his dad in a cab uptown. Everything he needs for the End is at Sandra's apartment, but he doesn't think he'll ever go back to get it. It doesn't matter anyway. Sandra can keep the beans, the water, the duct tape, the lock. Even Jennifer's photographs. None of it will bring his sister back.

Fifty-Seven

As gray light seeps between the blinds, Carol extracts herself carefully, scooting inch by inch toward the edge of the mattress. Her necklace chain is twisted, the ladybug charm digging into her chest. She finds her skirt and panties under the bed, her top and bra flung over the couch, her boots and Jennifer's blue suede jacket piled on a chair next to the door. Her hose are nothing but shreds. She throws them away.

The cross earrings are nowhere to be found.

Back in the bedroom, she leans down and breathes in the sour warmth of his breath. She picks up the pillow, still indented with her shape, and holds it above his head.

She can't do it; she can't be sure.

Hugging the pillow to her stomach, she takes three long breaths. She has done too much, gone too far already.

She lifts the pillow high and brings it down over Marcus's face.

For a moment, nothing happens. She pushes harder.

His body buckles. His hands come up, clawing at the pillow, slapping at her hands, his nails scratching her skin, drawing blood. She struggles to keep hold. Her blood runs down her hand, onto the white sheet, as he fights for his life.

Fifty-Eight

"Hello," Drew shouts as he opens the apartment door, not expecting a response, receiving none. Ben starts toward his bedroom.

"Wait," Drew says. "Come here a moment."

In the living room, Drew pushes apart the curtains, letting in the weak morning light. Ben flops down on the couch. Drew pats his feet, and he lifts them, making a place for Drew to sit.

Drew takes the notebook out of his shirt pocket and turns it end over end between his hands. "This is something I made for Jennifer," he says. "I'd like you to have it."

Ben sits up. "What is it?"

"Read it. You'll see."

"Okay." Ben takes the notebook. "Thanks."

"You should sleep. I'll make breakfast."

"*You'll* make breakfast?"

"Sure," Drew says, "I've made one or two in my life."

But they both just sit there.

"How did you find out," Ben says, "about Jennifer?"

Drew rubs his hands together; this is the conversation he least wants to have, but he knows it is necessary. "I identified her body," he says.

"When?"

"Today." But it's a different day now. "Yesterday."

"Her body," Ben says.

"Your mother and I. We wanted to believe she was alive."

"I did, too."

"But you couldn't."

"I felt it." Ben presses the center of his chest. "Right here."

"You didn't say anything."

"How could I do that to you and mom?"

Drew looks at his son sitting next to him—his sweet child, beautifully flawed.

"You should get some sleep," he says again, and this time Ben gets up and goes to his room.

Drew wanders the apartment, feeling like a visitor, every room strange now, distorted. In their bedroom, Carol's closet door is ajar, but nothing else has changed. He stares at the clothes on their hangers, but it's impossible to tell what's missing, which items Carol chose, where she has worn them. On the floor he finds her cell phone, the battery dead. He plugs it in, along with his phone, charging side by side.

Standing beside the desk in Jennifer's old room, he opens the blinds and looks out. The concrete alley, Dumpsters and fire escapes, the corner of a neglected backyard garden. He doesn't remember ever looking out this window before. He regrets changing around the room, getting rid of Jennifer's things; he wants something of hers to hold on to, but for now, this view will have to be enough.

In the kitchen he starts the coffee and thinks about Jennifer's body, lying somewhere in the medical examiner's office, waiting again for him to rescue her. Soon, he tells her. After the autopsy has been completed, he will go get his little girl. He will meet with a funeral director, buy a casket, prepare a ceremony, making everything as nice as it can be. He will bury her next to his parents in Calvary Cemetery and place flowers on her grave, rake off the leaves in the fall, scrape off the snow in the winter. He will take good care of her. If he can do nothing else, he can promise her that.

In the refrigerator the pickings are slim, but he finds eggs, milk. He decides to make pancakes. He has never made them before; they might turn out to be a disaster, but when his wife and son sit down at the table, he will have something to give them.

———

Ben's dresser drawers are open, the contents of the middle one spilled all over his bed. His desk drawer is open, too, his magazine on top. Shit. He can't think about that right now.

He shoves his clothes onto the floor and lies down. As exhausted as he is, he can't fall asleep. His mind races, going over the night, remembering all the moments he most wants to forget.

On his wrist, the *J* or *S* has smeared, the ink barely visible.

He rolls over and opens the notebook his dad gave him. He begins to read.

———

The sky transitions to blue as Carol walks uptown. Cabs pull up alongside her, but she is not ready to get inside, not yet. She needs to feel the pavement beneath her feet, the chill in the morning air, so that she understands that she is still here, among the living.

Her hand has stopped bleeding, but the scratches throb. She'll need soap and water to wash away the streaks. Somehow she will have to get to the bathroom before Drew and Ben see.

Drew will be angry. She won't be able to explain.

After three blocks she takes off the ladybug charm, tosses it and the chain into the street. The action does little to absolve her.

"I'm sorry, sweetie," she whispers, hugging herself inside Jennifer's jacket. "I'm so, so sorry."

One foot in front of the other, and soon she will be home.

ACKNOWLEDGMENTS

I am grateful to Kate Johnson for her faith in this book and determination in finding it a good home; Vivian Lee and everyone at Little A for being that home and making me feel at home in the process; my early readers, David Burr Gerrard, Olena Jennings, and Ryan Joe, for pushing me to turn the story into a novel; and my teachers, students, and wider community of writers for providing constant education and inspiration.

Eric—it's very useful to have a husband with a sharp editorial eye. Thank you for all that you do.

And Owen—you came into the world during the making of this book and transformed me into a mother. Every word I write will always be for you.

ABOUT THE AUTHOR

Courtney Elizabeth Mauk is the author of the novels *Orion's Daughters* and *Spark*. She lives in New York City with her husband and son.